When did business become pleasure?

He pulled her hand back so that she turned in his direction. "I want to get to know your city better. And I especially want to get to know you better." He swung her arm back again. "That's why I kidnapped you from the party." His tone was jovial, despite his words.

Carly played along. "You make it seem rather ominous."

"I might as well be honest," he said, "I have every intention of—"

Warnings flashed in her head. Before he could finish the sentence, Carly interrupted. She worried that Richard mistook her permission for him to take her home as an invitation for him to behave the way he had the other day. "I only want to be friends, nothing more."

"That's going to be extremely difficult. You must know by now that I'm attracted to you."

PHYLLIS HUMPHREY's knowledge of the stock market was evidenced in her book *Wall Street on $20 a Month: How to Profit from an Investment Club.* She is also the author of six romance novels, several short stories, and many articles in national magazines. She's active in her church, is a member of Mensa, and is listed in *Who's Who in the West 1997.* After raising four children, she and her husband live in Southern California.

Books by Phyllis Humphrey

HEARTSONG PRESENTS
HP142—Flying High

Charade

Phyllis Humphrey

Heartsong Presents

A note from the author:

I love to hear from my readers! You may correspond with me by writing:

> **Phyllis Humphrey**
> **Author Relations**
> **PO Box 719**
> **Uhrichsville, OH 44683**

ISBN 1-58660-612-3

CHARADE

All scripture quotations, unless otherwise indicated, are taken from the HOLY BIBLE, NEW INTERNATIONAL VERSION®. NIV®. Copyright © 1973, 1978, 1984 by International Bible Society. Used by permission of Zondervan Publishing House. All rights reserved.

All of the characters and events in this book are fictitious. Any resemblance to actual persons, living or dead, or to actual events is purely coincidental.

Cover illustration by Dick Bobnick.

one

On a scale of one to ten, Carly Jansen decided her office space on the main floor of the Wilson, Phelps, and Smith brokerage firm ranked about a four. Partitions, rather than interior walls, separated her office cubicle from the others. Furnishings included a desk, two chairs, a computer, and a telephone. She really didn't need anything more—other than another client or two. Even so, she felt this was the right occupation for her, and if she worked hard, more clients would show up soon.

She studied her list of "possibles." However, before she could reach for the phone to call the first one on the list, a deep bass voice greeted her.

"Good morning."

Carly lifted her gaze to see a man standing at her cubicle's entrance. Tall and well built, the man had dark brown eyes and hair a darker shade of red than hers. He wore a striking Burberry raincoat.

She couldn't help smiling. The man must not be a native. True San Franciscans seldom wore raincoats in June. The morning fog would soon burn off, no matter how gloomy the weather seemed at the moment.

"May I help you?" she asked.

"I'm looking for a stockbroker." He shrugged his broad shoulders. "The receptionist pointed me in this direction, but I thought she sent me to a Carl Jansen."

"It's Carly Jansen, and you're in the right place. I am a registered representative." Her husband, Brett, had worked here before her, but after he had been struck by a car and killed, she'd been persuaded to take his place.

The towering stranger stood, unmoving, in her doorway. She guessed him to be well over six feet tall. Carly managed a quick survey of his angular and incredibly good-looking face, with its aristocratic nose and straight lips. She couldn't help but wonder how this redhead could tan so well. She had never been able to achieve such a feat.

"I was expecting—" he began, then paused.

"A man," Carly finished for him. "I'm sorry to disappoint you, but there are many women representatives these days. And besides," she added with a broad smile, hoping to convince him to stay, "it's my turn."

"I beg your pardon?" He stepped forward, filling her small office space with his imposing presence.

"Please sit down," Carly invited, pointing to one of the two walnut armchairs opposite her desk. "The receptionist directed you to me because each representative is called, in turn, when a new client comes into the office."

The man continued to stand, so Carly rose as well. Even at five feet nine in her heels, she had to look up to him.

"I see," he answered and then repeated, "It's your turn."

"Exactly."

"I don't mean to appear chauvinistic, but I had been expecting a man, and. . ." His words trailed to silence.

At least he had the decency to appear embarrassed about his remark. "I assure you I'm perfectly capable," Carly said. "Women take the same course of study for these positions as men and must turn in equally high marks."

"It's not that," he said, then added, "You're so young."

"Thank you for the compliment, but I'm almost thirty." She hadn't lied. Twenty-eight *was* a lot closer to thirty than it was to twenty. She had learned her first week on the job that people in their thirties and forties—she judged this man to be somewhere in between—had difficulty accepting investment advice from someone too many years their junior.

"Please be seated," she said again.

He continued to stare at her until she could feel a flush rising to her usually fair skin. "Excuse me," he said after an uncomfortably long pause. Then he turned and left.

She watched him return to the receptionist and engage in a brief conversation before marching off in the direction of the manager's office. A shiver of consternation swept over her as she thought about how the man had simply rejected her out of hand. She could only imagine what he was saying to her boss right now.

She sank down into her chair before any coworkers could speculate as to why she was staring over the partition toward the manager's office. No matter how offensive the man's actions, she knew she must forgive him for his behavior. Bitterness hurt only the person who held onto such negative thoughts.

Obviously, this man was not the right customer for her. If he was not to be her client, then it could only mean that other—better—clients would soon come along. She knew she could trust God enough to direct and provide for her.

She also knew work proved to be the best remedy for despair, so she turned her attention once more to the list of names on her desk. Yet her mind refused to concentrate. The print blurred before her eyes. She could think only of the man now in her boss's office—the man who was, no doubt, talking about her.

Bill Trask, the manager of this branch of Wilson, Phelps, and Smith, was more than her employer. He was her friend. She and Brett had often invited Bill to dinner. They had also sailed with him on his twenty-eight-foot boat in San Francisco

Bay. Fifteen years older than Carly and divorced for the past few years, he had taken an almost fatherly interest in her since Brett's death a little over a year ago. Bill was the one who had urged her to join the firm.

Still, friends or not, she was not a charity case and would never let him down. She had thrown herself into studying the market and found that she not only liked the world of buying and selling securities but apparently had an aptitude for it.

Once she acquired a long list of satisfied customers and began to generate high commissions for the firm, Bill would see his decision to hire her justified and would be proud of her. Certainly, if hard work was any criterion for success, she would attain that goal before she reached the age of the man who had just left her office.

As if responding to her unspoken thoughts, the man himself once more appeared in her doorway. Her lower lip dropped in surprise, and her eyes widened.

"Ms. Jansen, please forgive my earlier rudeness." He removed the coat he wore over a well-cut business suit, placed it carelessly across the back of the chair, and sat down.

Still shocked, Carly didn't answer. Besides, his earlier dismissal remained too fresh in her mind.

"You must have thought my remarks were based on your being a woman. That wasn't the case at all," he said, studying her intently. "It was merely a misunderstanding."

Carly felt more than a little uncomfortable under his scrutinizing gaze, but she refused to look away.

"Mr. Trask has been telling me how qualified you are," the man continued. "Head of your class. Graduating with high honors from Stanford University. A member of Mensa. I must say, I'm very impressed."

At his words of compliment, her hurt melted like ice cream in the summer sun. Carly felt grateful for his changed attitude.

He looked and sounded sincere. " Mr. Trask was kind to give me such a recommendation."

"I explained to him that I was just moving to town from the East Coast and came to your offices looking for a local broker to handle my investments. Mr. Trask said you recently prepared an outstanding report, and that you have a real grasp of the market. Besides—" He hesitated, then added, "I have my aunts to consider."

"Your aunts?" Carly repeated.

"Yes, they live in this area and apparently worked with your late husband, Brett Jansen. They told me to look him up."

Carly's rising spirits dropped once again. So he hadn't chosen her for her expertise after all, but merely because his aunts were satisfied with Brett's performance. Reminding herself to be gracious, she kept a professional manner. "What are their names?"

"Mary and Martha Kemper."

Carly reached for her client book and scanned the list. "I contacted them, but they never returned my calls."

"Perhaps they didn't recognize the name. They're elderly ladies and sometimes a little. . ." He paused. "They might not have made the connection between Brett and Carly Jansen."

"But the fact is," she said, "I am not my husband. Perhaps, now that you know your aunts didn't recommend me at all, you'd prefer to see someone else."

As soon as she said the words, Carly regretted them, and inwardly she chastised her sudden reluctance. She needed new clients. She certainly shouldn't be encouraging a prospect to go elsewhere.

He studied her face before answering. "Had that been the case, I wouldn't have returned to your desk. But here I am."

Carly found his gaze unnerving, and his eyes seemed to bore into her. She looked away, trying to cover her unexpected confusion. Then, taking a deep breath, she reached into her desk drawer for a new client form to fill out and plunged ahead. "Very well, Mr. Kemper."

"Davis. My aunts' names are Kemper, but mine is Davis."

"I'm sorry."

"No apology necessary. I should have made that clear at the outset. They're my mother's sisters and never married." His gaze swept over her face. "In spite of my earlier reluctance, Ms. Jansen, I think this can be a very rewarding experience."

Carly's gaze flew to him once more and she tried to read the meaning of his words in his expression. *If he is expecting. . .* She stopped herself.

Surely her own vulnerability made her assume that every casual remark held some innuendo. During her first few months of widowhood, male acquaintances—even husbands of some of her friends—had tried to comfort her in ways that were inappropriate, as if a love affair with them would be sufficient to overcome her grief. As a result, now she suspected every man she met as having ulterior motives.

Carly forced her suspicions aside. Mr. Davis didn't seem like the kind of person who would make such a proposition. He appeared serious and businesslike, just the sort of client she wanted. "Your first name?" she asked, pen poised over the form.

"Stuart, but I usually go by Rich—short for Richard, my middle name."

Again, Carly's personal thoughts intruded. She liked the name Richard, had often thought she would give a son that name when she had children. She shook her head slightly as though to push the personal musing from her mind.

"Will there be any other names on the account?" she asked.

"No. I'm single," he replied, without volunteering any further explanation.

After filling in his address, telephone number, and other required information, she put down her pen and asked the most important question. "What are your investment objectives, Mr. Davis?"

"Capital appreciation. I have no need for present income. As a matter of fact, I prefer not to have large dividends which are taxable. Not in my tax bracket."

"Are you interested in municipals?"

"Definitely not. Bonds of any kind are far too tame." His face turned from serious to smiling, revealing even, white teeth, and his eyes seemed to twinkle with mischief. "I'm looking for growth, and I'm willing to be a little aggressive."

She liked his smile. She had already forgiven him for his earlier remarks. "A shade speculative, perhaps?"

"Yes, I don't mind taking a flyer now and then into a new company that might turn out to be another Microsoft. In fact, I discussed that with your manager a few minutes ago. He assured me you wouldn't be too conservative for my needs."

"I hope that's true." Carly remembered how her mother often lamented about having a red-haired child—impetuous and inquisitive from her earliest years.

"As a matter of fact, I do have a very interesting possibility. It's called Vickers Technology. It went public only two years ago." She looked up to see him frowning. "Is something the matter?"

"That's the electronics firm in what you call Silicon Valley, isn't it? Forget it. I'm not interested."

His manner was abrupt, and Carly felt her earlier antagonism returning. "I beg your pardon," she said. "I've investigated the company, and it's not one of those dot-com startups that—"

"I'm sorry," he interrupted, "but I happen to know their stock isn't going anywhere."

Carly was taken aback, but she managed to speak softly. "May I ask where you get your information? Since you've only recently moved to this area—"

"A friend of mine knows—"

"In other words, a tip," Carly said.

He paused before answering. "That's true, but—"

"It's your decision of course." She felt a little miffed but tried to remain objective. "I don't want to force you into anything against your better judgment."

"No one ever does," he said, and he seemed to have added a different quality to his tone of voice.

Carly found herself on the defensive. She knew this was one of her faults, but at the moment she wrestled with wanting to prove herself. "But," she protested, "our research department did a very thorough study of Vickers recently, and I visited their offices not two weeks ago for a firsthand look."

Still smiling, he leaned forward slightly. "Did you?" He suddenly seemed to be willing to listen to her opinions.

Carly took advantage of his new attitude to add arguments to her side. "Since you said you were interested in aggressive investing—even speculative, perhaps—I don't see how you can object to Vickers Technology."

"Perhaps you're right."

Despite trying to achieve this result, Carly was surprised by what seemed like Mr. Davis's somewhat sudden capitulation. A little flustered, she opened her file on Vickers Technology and focused on the papers inside.

"I predict," she said, "that their next quarter's earnings will be fifty percent higher and at a price/earnings ratio of only fifteen."

"Well, in that case, perhaps I'll try it." He raised one hand and pushed back a shock of hair from his forehead. "I could risk a gamble, a small one perhaps."

"I don't consider this a gamble. It could really be the growth company of the decade." She shut the folder.

He watched her, seemingly focusing his attention on her mouth. She bit her lower lip. For a long moment, words refused to come to her mind at all. Instead, she found herself looking at his mouth too. He had a generous mouth, with smooth, firm lips. An inquisitive smile pulled up at one corner.

Carly felt compelled to raise her gaze to meet his, and he blatantly stared back at her. Since Brett's death, she found admiring looks hard to deal with. A part of her knew she was expected to date. Even remarry. Yet another part of her refused to even consider the possibility.

She tore her gaze away and busied her hands by folding the *Wall Street Journal*, which lay open on her desk. Not since her first dates with Brett on the Stanford campus in Palo Alto had she felt sensations like this rushing through her. She took a deep breath. She wouldn't let herself be attracted to this man. It was still too soon. Her grief was still too fresh.

"Perhaps I've been a bit hasty in my decision. You see, I've just left my old job and came to San Francisco to make a new start, new city, new stock broker. I guess I can take a chance on a new company. Yes, I'll buy some—since you guarantee it's a good deal."

Guarantee? His remark brought her back to reality. "Mr. Davis, you're a knowledgeable investor. You know there are no guarantees in the stock market. We can only study past performance and consider possible future prospects."

"But you were so positive about it a moment ago. Are you revising your opinion?" He leaned back in the chair again, shifting his weight, his long legs stretched out in front of him.

"Not at all. I just meant—"

"Mr. Trask assured me that he hired you because of your

splendid qualifications, and you've studied the company. Why the doubt?"

His mention of Bill brought a different kind of doubt to Carly's mind—that she was their "token woman," hired merely to meet a female office quota. Yet she knew that wasn't true. In spite of their long friendship, Carly felt certain Bill had not hired her out of either pity or political correctness.

She raised her chin and straightened her back. "Very well, Mr. Davis, buy some shares in this company, and if they haven't increased in value within six months, I'll repay your brokerage commissions personally."

Her words seemed to come from some other person. Their rashness only began to penetrate her mind after they left her lips. She couldn't imagine what had made her say such a thing.

The room became ominously quiet. In the stillness, she regretted her outburst. Once again, her defensiveness had caused trouble. She said a quick prayer to help her overcome this fault. As for the moment, she tried to reassure herself that her offer couldn't be too disastrous. He had said he might invest only a very small amount in the company, just as a gamble.

The silence stretched. His searching gaze traveled up and down as he studied her. She fingered the collar of the camel-colored blouse that matched her suit. Somehow it seemed inappropriate today. Yet, she could hardly work in a down-town office wearing a muumuu or some other all-concealing garment. Besides, she was expected to conform to the same clothing styles as her clients.

Mr. Davis suddenly leaned forward, extended his hand to seal the bargain. He flashed her a broad smile.

"You have a deal, Ms.— See here, I can't call you Ms. Jansen. We're going to be very close from now on. I'll call you Carly instead. And you must call me Rich. Everybody does."

His strong hand dwarfed hers, but it was smooth, as if he had never done any physical labor. His touch sent disturbing sensations through her, and she pulled away as soon as she could do it politely. She swiveled her chair to face the small computer terminal in the corner, where she typed in the stock symbol of Vickers Technology. Its chart appeared on the screen.

"The current price is twenty-nine and a half," she quoted, using every ounce of her strength to remain riveted on business. "How many shares would you like?"

"Whatever fifty thousand will buy," he said.

A volcano erupted in Carly's chest. Fifty thousand dollars! Why, the commission on that was—was— Her mouth opened in surprise. Once more, she could only stare, speechless, at Mr. Davis.

"Are there not enough shares outstanding?" he asked, his eyebrows arching inquisitively. "It's not a thin stock, is it?"

"No, no," she murmured. Her face felt hot, and she was certain it was as red as her hair. "I mean, yes, there are enough," she stammered. She had all but memorized the statistics earlier, yet now she hardly knew what she was saying.

"Good." He stood up and flung his coat over his arm. "It's been a pleasure meeting you. I have no permanent daytime telephone yet, but you can reach me evenings at the number I gave you."

She rose when he did and said good-bye in a voice barely above a whisper.

He thrust his hand forward, and Carly reached out to shake it. Despite her self-denial of any physical attraction between the two of them, at his firm touch, an electrifying current raced up Carly's arm. He released her, turned, and left. She watched him walk through the office. He paused to look up at the electronic stock board with its moving letters and numbers; then he plowed through the doors and disappeared.

❧

Rich Davis hailed a cab on Montgomery Street. After telling the driver where he wanted to go, he sank into the upholstered back seat and envisioned the woman he had just met. The word *knockout* sprang to mind.

Perfect features, a great figure, and that short curly hair that formed a coppery halo around her face. He'd convinced himself he preferred women with long blond hair, certainly not a redhead like himself. He had always hated his own hair when he was a child. Hated being called "Red" or "Carrot-top." Fortunately, he'd been able to joke about it himself. Then, he'd grown tall enough that even such mild bullying stopped.

But Carly Jansen. . .

He could see it was going to be a pleasure to work with her. Of course, his business came first, and depending on what Ms. Jansen knew and when she knew it, she might not appreciate his interest in her at all. Still, he had a job to do. And he would keep his word, no matter what the cost.

two

Trying to sort out what had just happened, Carly stared at the glass double doors for several long moments after Rich Davis disappeared through them. Then she caught a glimpse of Bill Trask reentering his office, and she remembered what Davis had said. The temper that went with her red hair flared momentarily, but she subdued it. As a child, she'd been impetuous—prone to a quick temper—but her mother's rebuke, the sermons at church, and her Sunday school lessons had taught her a quick temper was not acceptable. If others behaved badly, that was their problem, not hers. Instead, she was to turn the other cheek, to love everyone, and to see them as God's perfect children.

Still, it wouldn't hurt to make Bill Trask proud of her by becoming the best representative that ever sat in this office. She turned back to her work.

In spite of the numerous telephone calls she made the rest of the morning, Carly found her new client intruding on her thoughts far too often. Was it merely because of her rash promise or because he had a magnetism that caused sensations she had not experienced since Brett's death? Perhaps it was the circumstances of their meeting and the mysterious aunts he mentioned who had worked with Brett. Odd that she didn't remember him ever saying anything about the ladies.

She reached into the file drawer of her desk and pulled out the folder marked "Kemper," again grateful that Bill had turned over some of Brett's clients to her. In fact, he had done his utmost to help her get started. Of course, not every one of Brett's clients had been referred to her. Some of them had very active accounts, and they had been turned over to other representatives in the firm. It had, after all, been a year since Brett's death; he couldn't expect customers to wait that long for someone to service their accounts, even if they were willing to switch to their previous broker's widow.

The Kemper file was thin. Obviously, it had not been a very active account. She saw very few transactions; all of them "buy" orders. And yet the ladies apparently were so impressed with Brett, they had urged their nephew to look him up. That seemed a little premature. Still, she supposed, elderly maiden ladies didn't always have to be logical.

She shrugged, returned the file, and glanced at her watch. The New York Stock Exchange would close in five minutes. Then she could have lunch and do some needed shopping.

A shadow appeared between her and the light, and looking up, she saw Bill Trask standing in her doorway.

She smiled. "Come in, Bill."

He dropped his plump figure into her extra chair and ran his fingers through his thick salt-and-pepper hair. "How's it going today, Carly?"

"That's an innocent question," she teased him. "It's quite obvious you're curious to know what happened with Mr. Davis."

"Well," he admitted, "I'm naturally interested. The man appeared somewhat irate when he reached my desk. I thought at first you'd been rude to him."

"Rude?" Carly was surprised he'd even think such a thing.

"Calm down," Bill soothed. "I soon learned the truth. He was looking for Brett, and the receptionist just caught the name 'Jansen' and directed him to you. He was surprised, that's all. I also detected a certain, shall we say, 'bias' in his tone."

" 'Bias' is putting it nicely," Carly answered. "And I must

thank you for your good comments on my behalf."

"I only told the truth," Bill continued. "You're a very bright lady, and I'm proud of your achievements here."

"Thanks again, but I wish I could reward your confidence with more clients than I've been able to produce so far."

"Give yourself time. You've only been here four months. Rome wasn't built in a day, you know."

Carly laughed. "What a clever saying. I must remember it."

Bill laughed with her. "I'm serious, though," he added. "Even Brett wasn't bringing in a decent commission check for the first year, as you of all people ought to remember."

"That's true."

"Be patient. Relax, and do the best you can. By the way," he added, after a pause, "you did land Davis, didn't you?"

Carly chuckled again. "Yes, I did, thanks in no small part to you." Her thoughts flew back to her promise to the man they were discussing, but she decided not to tell Bill about that, at least not yet. "It may not have been my expertise that did it, however, but your very kind remarks, along with a strong recommendation from his two maiden aunts."

"Maiden aunts? That's a new one." He got up to leave, then turned back. "By the way, you are coming to my house-warming Saturday, aren't you?"

"Yes, in fact I'm actually going shopping this very afternoon to buy a new dress for the occasion."

"I'm flattered."

She hadn't bought one in over a year, and she remembered the last formal occasion she had attended. Of course, she had been with Brett. She pushed the memory away. "I'm anxious to see your new townhouse."

The ringing of the telephone interrupted them, and Carly excused herself and picked it up.

"Miss Mary Kemper on line five," the operator said.

Wide-eyed, Carly looked across at Bill. Then she covered the mouthpiece with her free hand and whispered, "Speak of the, er, angels, one of Mr. Davis's maiden aunts is on the phone now."

Bill made the "okay" sign with his thumb and forefinger and left her office. Carly spoke into the telephone. "Put her through."

❧

Half an hour later, Carly was not shopping as she had expected. Instead, she stood in the lobby of the Greenhouse Restaurant, eagerly scanning every woman who entered. She was not kept waiting long. Two short, doll-like ladies approached her. They wore identical coats, with identical small hats perched on identically coifed gray hairstyles, above identical faces—twins in every sense of the word.

The one on the left spoke first. "Mrs. Jansen, I believe. I'm Mary Kemper. This is my sister—"

"Martha Kemper," said the lady on the right. "We're very glad to meet you. Richard did an excellent job of—"

"—describing you," finished Mary Kemper. "Shall we be seated? We don't usually wait this long for—"

"—our lunch," Martha concluded.

Carly's gaze bounced back and forth between the two ladies. They couldn't have resembled their nephew less, being as petite as he was tall, with almost pure white hair, and piercing blue eyes, whereas Richard's hair was a deep mahogany red and his eyes a soft brown. However, Carly recognized in his even, handsome features a hint of the ladies' faded beauty. Although the women's mouths were definitely more feminine, Carly noted a shared resemblance with their nephew's lips. Age had not pinched the twins' faces nor thinned their lips, although she guessed them to be at least in their seventies.

The hostess appeared, and Carly pulled her gaze away

from her luncheon guests to allow them to be led into the restaurant.

The sun shone through the whitewashed greenhouse ceiling of the main room, casting a pale glow on the white bamboo kiosks and the room's jungle-like profusion of tropical plants. The round table they were offered had a glass top under colorful place mats and napkins with a print that matched the chair cushions. Red anthuriums bloomed in a white vase in the center of the table. The three women quietly studied their menus, and after the waitress delivered three glasses of ice water, they placed their order.

"Well," Mary said when the waitress turned and walked away, "it's time we got better—"

"—acquainted," Martha added. "We were informed of your husband's death and that you were handling the account, and we ought to have—"

"—called you at once to express our sympathy."

Carly switched her gaze back and forth between the two ladies as they spoke, puzzling over their strange manner of conversation. Did they always finish one another's sentences this way? And how would she ever tell them apart? She couldn't expect Mary to be always on her left and Martha on her right to know who was who.

"Richard told us," Mary was saying, "that you are a remarkably beautiful young lady, and we must say—"

"—he was right," Martha concluded. "He's never been partial to redheads before. He hated his own hair color when he was a boy, you know—"

"—I think that was probably his reason—"

"—but I don't think that's important now," Martha interrupted her sister. "Let's get on with—"

"—what we came for? Very well. It's about our portfolio."

For the next hour, as they ate lunch, Carly continued to

turn first to one and then the other, hardly getting a word in herself as the two women told her about their investments. So far as she could make out, Mr. Davis knew very little about his aunts' private business. As their only living relative, he was their heir, and they didn't consider it proper that he learn their true worth. "Not that he is in any way eager to do so," Mary had hastened to say.

"Heavens no," Martha chimed in. "The boy hasn't a greedy bone in his body. In fact, how he managed to accumulate so much money himself—"

"—when he had no interest in business or finance in his youth," Mary finished, "has always been a wonder to us."

Their reluctance to discuss it with him stemmed from their upbringing. "In our day," Martha explained, "nice people did not discuss money." Nevertheless the ladies took a kind of impish delight in putting theirs to unusual uses. It amazed Carly to learn they had once owned a racehorse, an oil well, and part of a prizefighter.

"In our younger days that was," Mary said, "when we were only seventy."

"We're eighty-five now," Martha added, "and only fit for tame things—"

"—like the stock market," Mary finished.

Tame or not, their methods of investing in the stock market were unique to say the least, and Carly was intrigued by them. As she wondered why Brett had never mentioned the ladies, they solved the riddle.

"We were not well acquainted with your late husband. We gave him only a few very small orders—"

"—just to test him, you see. And then, when we were sure he was the soul of discretion, he—"

"—had that unfortunate accident. But Richard says—"

"—that you are a person to be trusted completely, and now

that we see you, we understand—"

"—what he meant perfectly," Mary finished.

Carly didn't know how the man could possibly have made such a decision in the brief time their conversation had taken. Still, there had been that occasional odd look on his face as he studied her. What quality had he found that made him call his aunts at once and tell them to contact her?

"But you see," Martha went on, "you must never tell Richard anything at all about what we buy and sell. You will keep this in strictest confidence—"

"—like a doctor or lawyer would."

"Naturally," Carly answered.

"That's why we didn't want to meet in your office," Mary said. "We'd like all of our discussions to be handled as discreetly as possible. No one must know what we're doing."

"I understand." Carly couldn't help wondering, however, just what kind of transactions they were going to want her to handle in the future. Like their nephew before them, they were making it sound quite mysterious. So far, the things they had mentioned were speculative, but far from dangerous. At any rate, they so obviously had their minds made up and had not asked Carly for advice that it would have been both rude and unethical for her to suggest they didn't know what they were doing with their own money.

"We'd like a thousand shares of First Imperial," Martha said.

Carly nodded. The stock was a fine, conservative investment.

But Mary's next words shocked her. "And will you please purchase a thousand shares of Vickers Technology for us—"

"—at the market tomorrow," Martha added.

Carly stopped writing in her notebook and looked up at them. "Are you sure? Vickers Technology?" Their nephew had obviously suggested the stock to them, but while it was all right for him—since he had suggested he wanted to invest in that type of stock—surely they were too old to do the same thing.

"Are you aware Vickers is a biotechnology company? That's a rather speculative investment for—" She stopped herself. She didn't want the age of the sisters to be the basis of her stock recommendations, lest she be accused of age discrimination. On the other hand, diligence required she inform her clients when she thought they were choosing inappropriate stocks.

"Yes," Martha repeated, "Vickers Technology. We know all about what they do. We like to be on the cutting edge. And now we shall say our good-byes."

While Carly pondered the modern phrase Martha had used, they rose from their chairs in unison, and Mary picked up the check that had just been deposited on the edge of the table.

Carly reached for it. "Please allow me."

"We wouldn't hear of it," Martha said. "You were our guest."

Still protesting mildly, Carly followed the ladies back to the entrance lobby, where Mary dropped the check on the counter and said to the cashier, "Put this on our bill, please." Then she turned, smiled at Carly, and said to her sister, "Shall we go, Dear?" Without another word, they left the building and climbed into a cab, which had conveniently appeared curbside on Taylor Street just as they emerged from the building.

three

As Carly drove south down the peninsula, she rehearsed the list of questions she would ask Len Vickers, the president of Vickers Technology. After her lunch with the Kemper twins, she had telephoned him for an appointment, wanting to hear again from his own lips the prospects of his company doubling its earnings by the end of the third quarter.

She'd had no doubts about the company on her previous trip. Her sudden fears for her judgment were the direct result, she knew, of Mr. Davis's aunts buying the stock, and of his accepting her rash promise to return his brokerage commissions personally if the stock didn't perform well.

There was no point in berating herself once more about her momentary lapse in sanity. She had said it and he had accepted her challenge. There was nothing to do now but accept her fate with as much grace as she could muster. In fact, there was really no point in going back to the firm again. She supposed it was a desire to assure herself she hadn't been completely absurd when she promised Davis that the earnings would rise.

She drove into the parking lot; then entered the air-conditioned office building. It seemed dark after being in the bright sunlight, and Carly stood at the reception desk a moment to let her eyes adjust.

"Please be seated," the receptionist said after Carly gave her name. "Mr. Vickers will be with you in a moment."

Carly headed for one of the chairs in the waiting area, but she startled when a man rose in front of her. Rich Davis.

"You!" she stammered. "What are you doing here?"

"The same as you, apparently," he answered, taking her hand in his. "And how are you this afternoon?"

Stunned into silence, Carly allowed him to lead her to a chair, wondering all the while if he could feel her wildly beating pulse. As she dropped into her seat, he released her hand and sat beside her. "I didn't expect to see you." He spoke in a soft, confidential tone. "Didn't you tell me in your office this morning that you had visited Len Vickers only two weeks ago?"

"Yes," Carly said, her face feeling uncomfortably warm under his searching gaze. "I did visit him recently."

"Then why are you back again? Is it possible you weren't as sure of your findings as you led me to believe?" His words were serious, but his eyes sparkled with merriment.

"No, it's not," she answered, her voice as low as his. "I have every confidence the company's earnings will double, just as I told you."

"Then why?"

She considered inventing some reason—perhaps telling him there was one other question she had wanted to ask that she'd forgotten before. But that would be a lie. She had to stop being so defensive, yet it was difficult to be totally professional when this man smiled at her the way he was doing now.

"Thank you for your interest, Mr. Davis," she said, "but my reasons for being here are—are—confidential." Well, that much was true. She'd been sworn to secrecy by his very own aunts.

"Please," he said as he reached for her hand again. "I thought we were going to be Carly and Rich."

"You may call me whatever you like, but you're my client, and I don't think I should be so informal." She pulled her hand free, as much to establish the distance between them as to hide the fact that her palm was hot and trembling from his touch.

Then she remembered her surprise at finding him there. "You asked about my reasons for being here. What about yours? Were you following me?"

"Not at all. Believe me, I'm as surprised as you are that we both turned up here this afternoon."

"So, why are you here? You seemed less than interested in the company this morning."

"I pride myself on being open-minded. Since you sounded so sure of your facts, I thought I might have been hasty in my first opinion. I decided to see for myself."

"In that case, perhaps I should leave." She started to rise, wondering why her emotions seemed so contrary. She wanted to stay, yet he seemed to confuse her.

He grasped her arm firmly. "Why do that? Let me be the one to leave."

"No, that isn't necessary. After all, I've visited the company before and you haven't. I really think you should talk to Vickers. I think he'll convince you just as he did me."

"I didn't mean to offend you. I really didn't think you would be upset by my coming here, even if you—"

"Even if I found out?" she finished. "But I'm not offended. You have every right to be here. Please don't think I'm upset."

"Look here—"

Whatever he was about to say was cut short by the approach of Len Vickers, a balding man in his late thirties, with horn-rimmed glasses, a thin face, and a tall, angular body.

"Hello, Mrs. Jansen," he said jovially. Then, turning to Davis, he said, "Rich, old man, it's good to see you again."

Carly felt a knot in her stomach. Just what was going on here? Davis had never even mentioned that he knew Vickers, much less that they were this friendly. Furthermore, for a while this morning, he had been unwilling even to consider their stock.

"You two know each other?" Vickers asked.

Carly had been about to ask the same question, but stopped. Since there was no good reason to leave now, she smiled politely at Vickers. "Mr. Davis and I met in my office this morning. He allowed me to persuade him to buy some stock in your company, and now, quite by chance, we both turned up here this afternoon."

"That's wonderful," Vickers said smoothly, apparently not concerned about who had persuaded whom. "I can take you both on a tour of the plant. You've never seen it, Rich, but I hope you'll be impressed."

As they surveyed the plant, Carly felt excluded from most of the conversation. They passed trough room after room of workers assembling parts. Through laboratories where white-coated men and women peered into microscopes. Through large, well-lighted offices filled with computers. All the while, Vickers explained procedures and answered questions posed by Carly's unexpected companion.

She didn't really mind. She'd had this tour before. So, even if she'd been able to, she didn't need to concentrate. Instead, she spent her time trying to understand why Davis had been so reluctant to consider Vickers' stock. She couldn't guess what game he was playing. And what about his two aunts and their games? The secrecy? Were all the people in his family so mysterious about their business?

Walking beside the tall, arrestingly handsome man, watching him, hearing him ask intelligent questions, she couldn't help but be impressed. She was aware, too, of something else. She felt as if more than coincidence brought them here at the same time. Her heart began to pound, and her skin tingled.

An hour after starting the tour, they stood, once again, in the lobby. After they said good-bye to Vickers, he returned to his office.

"May I drop you somewhere?" Davis asked her.

"No, I have my own car."

He held open the door for her, and she started across the parking lot. To her surprise, he followed.

"Then could you drop me?" he asked.

"I beg your pardon?" She stopped and they almost collided.

"I don't have a car yet," he said. "I came down on the Southern Pacific and then took a cab."

After a pause, she said, "Of course, I'll gladly give you a ride back." Resuming her walk to her blue Ford Escort, she told herself she was only being polite. Yet, she couldn't keep from feeling glad about extending her time with him. She couldn't deny the sudden lift in her spirits. "Where are you staying in the city?"

"I'm at the Fairmont, but I'm looking for an apartment or house to rent. Eventually, I'd like to buy some property."

Carly didn't answer but unlocked the car door, and he held it open for her. She felt uncomfortably aware of his watching her as she settled herself in the driver's seat. Then he went around and got in beside her. She felt all thumbs as she inserted the key in the ignition and started the car. She maneuvered it out of the parking space and into the traffic that was building for the evening commuter rush.

"I'm very impressed with Vickers Technology," he said finally, breaking a rather lengthy silence.

"Are you really?"

"I have the feeling you doubt me," he answered lightly. "Where have I gone wrong?"

"For openers, how about that little charade in my office this morning? Pretending you didn't know anything about Vickers?" Carly waited for his reply, her gaze straight ahead.

After a pause he said, "I guess that was rather foolish of me. You're far too perceptive a person to be taken in. At any rate, you would have found out sooner or later."

"Found out what?"

"Let's keep it for later, shall we?"

"What is it you're hiding?" She was a bit annoyed with his secrecy. "If it's anything I ought to know about, anything illegal or unethical about the company—"

"No, no," he assured her, "nothing like that. You'll have to trust me. I wouldn't do anything to hurt you."

His choice of words made Carly even more suspicious. What did he mean by not "hurting" her? Somehow that made it sound as if there were more at stake than money.

"I suppose I can't force you to tell me what it is," she said, keeping her voice even. "The broker-client relationship ought to be one of mutual trust and confidence. As you know, millions of dollars' worth of stock change hands every day with only a verbal agreement."

"I'm aware of that. Again, all I can say is that I haven't told you any lies. I never said I didn't know Len Vickers. You just have to believe me when I say you have nothing to fear."

Frustrated, Carly realized her foot was pressing too heavily on the accelerator, and she lifted it. She forced herself to relax, telling herself she might as well not worry about it since she could do nothing anyway.

She intentionally changed the subject. "How long have you been in San Francisco?"

"A little over a week."

"How do you like it so far?"

"It's all that I expected and more," he answered. "I've been to California before, but never to Frisco. I must say it's every bit as charming as I'd been led to believe."

"Excuse me, but let me caution you never to say Frisco," Carly corrected him. "You immediately stamp yourself as an outsider. It goes back to the early days of the city. During the gold rush, San Francisco was a rather bawdy place. Since the miners called it Frisco, the men who made their money in railroads, banking, and other more respectable ways made it a point not to use the expression. Most residents have not used it from that day to this."

"How interesting," he said with a chuckle. "You are a virtual storehouse of San Francisco history."

Carly couldn't help smiling. "Not really. But frankly, I do find it fascinating."

"I'll look forward to hearing more one day."

Again, Carly flashed a suspicious look at her passenger as she tried to decipher his meaning. His next words removed all doubt.

"Will you have dinner with me tonight?"

"I—no. I'm sorry. I get up extremely early, because of the New York Stock Exchange opening three hours ahead of us."

"It's not even six o'clock. And you have to eat sometime. I don't mind dining early if that's better for you."

Carly considered it. On one hand, she enjoyed his company and felt reluctant to end the moment. Yet she was nervous. She had been out with a man only once since Brett's death and that was with the brother of an old school chum who happened to be in town. With her unusual hours, she couldn't keep late nights anyway. But this time, she had a sensation of being somehow disloyal to Brett's memory to have anything resembling a date.

Still silent, Carly saw her exit approaching and pulled off the freeway onto the city streets. The heavy traffic forced her to creep along, inching her car toward Nob Hill.

"You didn't answer my question," he reminded her as they finally neared the hotel. "What are you afraid of?"

Afraid? No, it wasn't that. She was always in control of herself and her emotions. Having dinner with a man was not necessarily an invitation to anything else.

"Very well," she said at last. "The Crown Room has a nice view, although no doubt you've seen it already."

"As a matter of fact, yes," he replied, "but it was dark at the time. I'm sure the view is different during the day."

"I'll park the car."

"Let the doorman do it for you." Rich stepped from the car, which Carly had stopped in the circular drive. He said a few words to the doorman, then held her door while she climbed out of the car. They crossed the lobby and took the elevator to the Crown Room, where they were shown to a window table. The clear skies afforded them a vast view of the city, the waters of the bay, and the hills beyond.

After they ordered, he relaxed in his seat and said, "Tell me about yourself."

"There's not much to tell," she answered. "I graduated from Stanford, as Mr. Trask told you. I married right out of college, and now I work in the brokerage office."

"Trask indicated your husband died rather tragically."

"Let's not talk about that." She looked away, unable to bear the painful memories of Brett's death. She composed herself, then asked, "What about you? You said you were from back East."

"Boston. I was born and raised there; then I attended a very small private college in the Midwest."

"That explains why you have no Eastern accent."

"I pick up accents wherever I am, but I think the Midwestern accent is almost universal in this country. However, if I spent ten days in Birmingham, Alabama, I suspect I'd go around saying 'y'all' like a native."

Carly laughed. She felt relaxation creep over her body. She couldn't decide whether it was her present company or the pleasant atmosphere that soothed her.

As if his intuition told him she felt more comfortable, he pressed her again for details about her life. "Did you major in business in college? Is that how one prepares for a career as a stockbroker?"

"Actually, I never expected to become a stockbroker. I majored in library science until I met Brett, and he convinced me to switch over." She realized she had spoken his name without flinching. "He was a great help to me."

"As you're a member of Mensa, I suspect that wasn't a big problem." A disarming smile made the lines around his eyes crinkle.

"You've heard of Mensa, then?"

"An organization for people with IQs in the top two percent of the population—about 133, I believe."

"You're very well informed." She fingered the bow of her blouse while she studied his face. She wondered what reason he might have had for remembering such a thing. "Are you a member too?"

"No, but I must say I never imagined that people of such high intelligence could also be beautiful and charming." He leaned across the table toward her as if to take her hand, but just then the waiter brought their dinner.

Carly was grateful for the interruption. She felt uncomfortable talking about herself. He was the mysterious one, and she had learned almost nothing about him. "What did you do after college?"

"I traveled around for a while. I like to think I hold the record for having stayed in the most youth hostels in Europe. Then I met a young woman and moved to New York." He paused and Carly feared he would say no more, so she prompted him.

"And?"

"Frances was an actress. Excuse me, Frances is an actress."

"She must be both beautiful and intelligent," Carly said. "Acting requires a lot of study."

"Actresses are not necessarily beautiful," he said, looking into her eyes. "In this case, however, it was true." After another pause, he continued without further urging. "I moved to New York to be near her while she pursued her career. That's when I became involved in investing on Wall Street. Then we broke up."

"Just like that?" Carly asked.

"Just about like that. She found her career more attractive than the idea of marriage." As if the subject were closed, he tackled his steak with vigor and she did the same, letting the background music replace their conversation.

Carly broke the silence. "She must be famous by now, your ex-girlfriend, that is. Would I have heard of her? Frances what?"

"She's not Frances anymore. She changed it to Ferris Gray, and last I heard, she was doing rather well." He shifted in his chair, as if uncomfortable talking about her.

Carly caught his mood. "I didn't mean to pry. As a matter of fact, I think I've heard of her. Didn't she have a part in that Chicago gangster film last year?"

"Yes, I believe she did. You have a remarkable memory if you can recall the names of the bit players."

"Oh, it was more than a bit part. But you're right, I do tend to remember things like that. Brett always accused me of stuffing my head with trivia."

She wondered why she'd brought up Brett's name again. Bill Trask had always told her not to block out his memory completely, that talking about him would eventually ease the pain, but she couldn't remember the last time she had referred to him in casual conversation.

"It's a pretty head," Davis said, once more leaning toward

her. "And the stuffing doesn't show at all."

They shared another laugh.

"What kind of investing did you do in New York?"

"Oh, we're not going to talk business, are we?" He turned his head to the view. The sky was darkening to shades of blue and purple. "I want to know more about your city. What do you do on your days off?"

"Clean my apartment," Carly joked. "When Brett and I first moved here, we did all the tourist things, rode the cable cars, took cruises to Sausalito and Alcatraz, hiked Mt. Tamalpais. On Sunday afternoons in the summer, we attended the free concerts in Stern Grove or Golden Gate Park."

"That sounds wonderful. Perhaps you and I could do some of those things together." He looked steadily into her eyes.

Carly turned off her memories and returned to reality. No, they would not do those things together. It was one thing to be able to have dinner with a man without guilt, or even talk about Brett without pain, but she had no intention of getting involved with anyone yet—certainly not a complete stranger, and a mysterious one at that.

"It's getting late," she said, ignoring the coffee the waiter set in front of them. "I really should go."

"If you must." He asked for the bill, signed it, and helped Carly from her chair. He walked with her to the lobby, tipped the doorman, and again helped her into the car. Then he went around and got in beside her.

Surprised, she looked over at him.

"A gentleman always sees a lady home. I'll take a cab back. Besides, I want to see where you live. Or did you have other plans?" He gave her a look of innocence.

"No, not unless you consider washing my hair a plan." She slipped the car into traffic and headed for her nearby apartment. "It's my early hours, remember?" Carly fell silent, her private thoughts going in circles, wondering why she alternately wanted, then didn't want to know this man better. Finally, she pulled into her garage, and they got out of the car and returned to the sidewalk. In the building's shadows, it was almost totally dark, and Carly could barely see his face.

"It's been an interesting day," he said. "Forgive the cliché, but I feel as if I've known you much longer than ten hours."

The balmy evening breeze ruffled Carly's hair. She, too, felt as if she had known him longer than ten hours. Perhaps she should apologize for her abrupt departure from the Crown Room—for her overreaction to his suggestion that they might go places together. After all, they were going to be business associates. He might not have meant anything by his remarks. He could merely want to be a friend.

She wondered if she wanted him for a friend—or something more.

He stepped closer. Somehow, she knew at once what would happen, yet she felt powerless to prevent it. His hands held her gently by the shoulders, his head lowered to hers, and he brushed her lips with a kiss.

Carly, defenses in place, pushed him away. "Mr. Davis—"

"Please," he said, "you were going to call me Rich."

She shook her head. "Since you're so insistent that we be on a first name basis, I'll call you Richard. But you mustn't—"

It was his turn to look surprised and his dark brows arched. "How did you know I actually prefer Richard over Rich?"

She was about to say, "Your aunts use it," but then she remembered the ladies' admonition that she keep their comments confidential. She returned, instead, to matter of the kiss.

"You're trying to change the subject," she said. "You really— I mean, we can't have a business relationship if you—"

"I'm sorry," he said, as if just realizing he'd overstepped the bounds. "It wasn't fair of me to try to kiss you, but I've wanted to do that ever since I met you this morning."

Since this morning? Carly's heart pounded. Yes, he was good-looking and apparently wealthy, but surely he didn't expect all women to be amenable to his advances. "I've enjoyed our dinner and conversation, but I simply can't—"

"I'm sorry," he said again, genuine dismay on his features. "Don't worry," he added. "I won't let it happen again. I don't want to jeopardize our—friendship. I'll be a perfect gentleman from now on."

Carly felt herself relax slightly. If he'd keep his promise, she needn't risk losing him as a client for the firm. That was what she cared most about.

"Good night," he said.

"Good night." She walked quickly up the steps, not waiting to see if he flagged down a cab at the corner.

four

Saturday was Carly's favorite day. When she was a child, she would be up early every Saturday, running across the backyard, out the wooden gate, and down the road to find her friends. Her unruly mop of bright hair bobbing, she would lead explorations through the meadows. Some Saturdays, they would put on a show or a circus. They would bring their dogs and cats dressed up in old clothes and put paper streamers on their doll carriages or bikes.

Suddenly Richard Davis came to her mind, and she found herself wondering what occupied him on Saturdays as a child. *What is he doing today?* The unbidden question sprang into her thoughts, which led to the memory of his kiss. She wished he hadn't done that. Richard was a client and if one were smart, one simply did not get involved with clients. Even if she wanted to—and, honestly, she had to admit a strong attraction to him—she could never become involved with anyone who might not share her beliefs in matters of faith.

She replaced the thought of Davis with Bill Trask. This was the day of his housewarming party in his new condominium on Cathedral Hill, and he had invited the representatives from the stock brokerage, as well as other friends. Carly looked forward to it and had bought a new dress. Blue as cornflowers, it had a long skirt, tiny cap sleeves, and a cowl neckline. She added high-heeled pumps and donned her velvet evening coat.

Bill arrived in his white Cadillac and picked her up in front of her apartment. She found it pleasant not to have to worry about finding a cab or a parking place if she drove herself. He helped her into the car. "You look stunning tonight."

"Give yourself an A-plus for making a gal feel special."

"Just because I'm picking you up, don't think I intend to take you home later. There are some eligible men coming tonight who ought to receive that honor."

"Thanks, but no thanks. I'll take a cab."

"I wish you'd find someone so you needn't attend parties alone. I loved Brett like a brother, but it's been a year."

"I know, but I'm not in any hurry. In fact, I may never marry again. Unlike you, I have no unpleasant memories of a failed marriage. My marriage was wonderful. I can't imagine anyone else who could ever make me so happy again."

Bill fell silent for a moment; then he continued softly. "I hope you're not idealizing Brett. He was a fine person, and I'm glad you were happy with him, but he wasn't perfect. No one is. You can be happy again. You ought to be. But if you start canonizing Brett, you'll never find anyone who will live up to your overblown mental picture of him."

Richard Davis's face flashed before Carly's eyes. She pushed aside the image at once, annoyed with herself. Even if she were to consider finding someone to take Brett's place, Richard Davis would not be in the running. He was too much of a puzzle, one she didn't think she wanted to unravel.

"Thanks for your concern," Carly said, placing her hand on Bill's arm. "But don't worry. I can take care of myself."

"Hmm. Maybe that's what I'm afraid of."

In the modern living room of his apartment, already filling with guests, he introduced her to a tall, attractive blond. "This is Elinor," he said. "I believe you know everyone else, don't you?"

So Bill had a new girlfriend. No wonder he was eager to

pair her off with someone. Carly greeted people, then leaned over to sample the canapés on the coffee table in front of a sofa.

"There are some hot ones in the dining room." The voice came from behind her, and she straightened to see Richard Davis. He wore a black tuxedo, black tie, and pleated white shirt. He seemed even taller than she had remembered.

"Hello." Her hands were occupied—one with a small plate and the other with a cheese-topped tidbit—so she couldn't shake hands with him. Yet even without his touch, she was reminded of his attempt at a good-night kiss the last time she had seen him. The mere remembrance of it made her face warm and her scalp tingle.

"You are even more beautiful than the last time I saw you, if that's possible," he said.

Carly paused before speaking. "Thank you. I see you're making friends in San Francisco quickly."

"Yes, Bill Trask was kind enough to invite me tonight. We had a nice chat yesterday."

"You weren't complaining about me again, were you?" she teased, remembering his first reaction when they met.

"By no means. In fact, we didn't mention you at all."

Carly was relieved. She had no wish for Bill to know they had been to Vickers Technology together—or of the following experiences they had shared that evening.

"I asked his advice about finding a place to live," Richard continued, "and he suggested I come tonight so that I could see this building. He says there are still a few units available."

"It's very attractive," Carly said, using the comment as an excuse to look around the room instead of into his eyes.

"It is indeed. I might like it as a San Francisco address."

"Just as a San Francisco address? Does that mean you aren't going to make this your permanent home after all?"

"The bay area, yes. I meant I might like a home in the suburbs. Marin County is lovely, and I could drive across the Golden Gate Bridge every day."

"It's just a bridge," Carly said. "We actually have several."

" 'Just a bridge'? You underestimate it. Perhaps you haven't traveled enough to know how unique it really is. In fact, the Bay Bridge has been described as 'merely a span.'"

"You seem to know a lot about the bay area all of a sudden. Have you been boning up?"

He smiled and Carly again felt her heart begin to beat strongly. Why did his smile always do that to her?

"My aunts," he said. "They've lived here most of their lives. Like you, they're veritable storehouses of information about San Francisco. I visited them most of the day."

Carly liked to think of him with the two eccentric ladies, sitting at their feet as they told him stories of the old city.

"However, I was rather hoping to learn more about San Francisco from you. I enjoyed our. . .conversation."

Carly changed the subject. "Didn't you say something about hot hors d'oeuvres in the dining room?" She moved away.

Richard didn't follow her. When next she saw him, he was in the middle of a small group and seemingly holding everyone spellbound with a funny story. After his audience laughed loudly, she approached and stood on the fringe, listening to the conversation. It had turned to local politics, and this time, others did most of the talking, while Richard listened attentively to whoever was speaking.

Eager to know her better, Carly found Elinor, and they enjoyed a lengthy talk. Then she saw Richard involved in still another group of interested listeners, both speaking and encouraging others to voice their own opinions. If she had worried that he might monopolize her all evening, she needn't have. He seemed totally comfortable with others, making friends and being the charming guest. Everyone seemed to like him.

Hours later, although it didn't seem very late, Bill announced that a friend of his, Tommy Purcell, had agreed to favor them with his piano playing. Carly recognized the man. Now in his fifties, he had once been an actor in Hollywood musicals but now played in a local nightclub. The Bobby Short of San Francisco, as it were. Carly moved close to the ebony grand piano in the corner of the living room.

Tommy played and sang some of the songs from his films, then launched into popular Broadway show tunes. Finally, he played well-known pop favorites and encouraged everyone to join him in the familiar words. Richard reappeared at Carly's side sometime during the sing-along.

When Tommy finally got up to leave, Richard joined in the heartfelt applause; then he took her arm. "May I take you home?"

Several other guests were thanking Bill for the lovely evening or heading for the guest room to pick up coats, so Carly let Richard get her wrap and hold it for her while she slipped her arms into the sleeves. When they approached Bill to say, "Good night," he smiled approvingly at them, as if it had been his plan all along that they should leave together. Carly couldn't very well ask Bill to drive her home now, so she accepted the arrangement.

When they reached the street, Richard said, "Do you mind if we walk?" Fresh cool air fanned Carly's face, carrying with it the scent of summer flowers, and she smiled her agreement. They walked down the slanted sidewalk that descended the hill, over curbs and across streets, his hand clasping hers securely. The city lights were beautiful, the air crystal clear, and the sky dotted with a million twinkling stars.

"Your city seems to have limitless charms," Richard said. "I can't decide if I prefer it in daytime or the evening."

"I feel that way sometimes myself."

"But you've always known it. I should think you'd be jaded by now. Or is San Francisco a city that never bores natives?"

"First of all, I'm not really a native. I was born in Pacific Grove and didn't come to the bay area until I received the scholarship to Stanford." They approached a street corner and Carly was grateful for Richard's hand in hers as they negotiated a rather steep curb.

"And secondly," she continued, "I think you're right. I do believe San Francisco is the only city where the residents enjoy it every bit as much as the tourists."

"That's a wonderful thing to say about a city."

"I hope I don't sound like someone from the Chamber of Commerce."

He pulled her hand back so that she turned in his direction. "I want to get to know your city better. And I especially want to get to know you better." He swung her arm back again. "That's why I kidnapped you from the party." His tone was jovial, despite his words.

Carly played along. "You make it seem rather ominous."

"I might as well be honest," he said, "I have every intention of—"

Warnings flashed in her head. Before he could finish the sentence, Carly interrupted. She worried that Richard mistook her permission for him to take her home as an invitation for him to behave the way he had the other day. "I only want to be friends, nothing more."

"That's going to be extremely difficult. You must know by now that I'm attracted to you."

"You made that clear Wednesday evening," Carly said, "but

we also agreed it wasn't wise to mix business with pleasure."

"Then you admit that our getting to know each other better could be a pleasure." He lifted one eyebrow and grinned.

Carly felt warm, her face tingled. "I didn't say that. I only meant we must keep our personal lives separate."

"I admit we haven't known each other very long, but people do meet and—in spite of convention—sometimes fall in love. You don't intend to live out your life as a lonely widow, do you?"

"Whether I do or not is really none of your business, you know. Please—" She pulled her hand from his and thrust it into the pocket of her coat. "—let's not talk about it."

She hadn't been paying attention to where they were walking, so Carly was surprised to realize they had come to a stop in front of her own building. She looked at Richard. "You certainly learned your way around the city in a hurry."

"Oh, didn't I tell you? I'm part homing pigeon."

"But this time it's *my* home."

"So much the better. You wanted to get here eventually, didn't you?" He took the key from her, unlocked the front door, and after they climbed the stairs, he unlocked her apartment door.

"Mind if I come in for just a minute?"

"Of course. I didn't mean you to think I'm hostile. We can be friends."

"Friends it is," he said, raising a hand. "I surrender to your wishes." He helped her out of her coat and draped it over a chair while she turned on lamps.

"I must get a car," he continued. "It was cruel of me to make you walk all this way."

"I didn't mind, although I think I'd like to take my shoes off." She smiled, glad he had changed the subject.

She stepped out of the high-heeled pumps, and he led her

to the sofa in front of the fireplace. "Do you mind if I light the logs?" After she nodded, he turned on the gas jet, and the logs began to glow.

"It's only a fake one." She felt foolish stating the obvious, but in spite of his lighthearted demeanor, she was beginning to feel odd again. She had been foolish to allow him in. She might find it hard now to convince him that she wanted no involvement if she let him share, even a brief time, in her private world. Somehow, she must keep everything impersonal. "Would you like something? Coffee, perhaps?" She started to rise.

"Nothing," he answered, and catching her hand again, urged her back into her seat once more. Instead of sitting next to her, however, he sat on the floor at her feet, his back against the sofa, his head near her knees. "Let's just enjoy the fire."

The silence felt comfortable. Reassuring. Friendly. She fought an almost irresistible urge to run her fingers through his thick, mahogany hair. Would it feel coarse or smooth?

"This is so peaceful," he said, "I could stay here forever." Then he turned around and looked at her.

She was amazed to see a sad look in his eyes. "What's the matter?" She felt a rising swell of emotion washing over her again.

He didn't answer, but the sadness in his eyes vanished. Graceful as a jungle cat, he unfolded his long frame from his position on the floor and sat beside her. One arm reached along the sofa back and stopped, inches from her shoulders.

"I can't remember when I've felt so comfortable."

She looked away. She must pull herself together. This was becoming far too dangerous. She could not become involved with this man. "You really ought to leave," she said. The words were automatic and she knew, even as she spoke, that neither she nor Richard would act on them.

Then he leaned toward her. His light kiss lasted no more than a moment.

"I'm sorry," he whispered as soon as he pulled back. "I shouldn't have done that, I know. I guess I got carried away."

The knot in her midriff intensified, and Carly could hardly think. She had spoken of keeping their relationship on a strictly friendship basis, yet she had not stopped him from kissing her. She blamed her reaction on any number of things—the evening, the way he behaved around her boss and his friends, the very way he looked, and the magnetism that emanated from him.

"You'd better leave." She rose from the sofa and walked softly across the room toward the door. He stole up behind her and stood close. Close enough to touch. Yet not touching her. He seemed to be waiting.

The words she wanted to say—a repetition of why they could not become emotionally entangled when they were to be business associates—lay behind her lips but refused to emerge.

He caressed her arms and laid his hands gently on her shoulders. Carly could feel his breath, warm on the back of her neck. With an ever-so-tender touch, he turned her toward him. He kissed her longer and with passion this time. She found no will to resist. He held her close. She put her arms around him.

Still holding her to him, he broke the kiss, and his voice became husky. "I've been attracted to you since the moment we met. When you looked so defensive and yet so adorable." He nuzzled her neck. "And then offering to repay my commissions. . ." His voice took on a lighter, humorous tone, with a deep chuckle. "You don't have to do that, you know."

At once, like a bubble bursting, the dreamlike sensations of the evening vanished. She regained control.

What had he said about the commissions she promised to repay? What did he mean when he said, "You don't have to do that"? Like a bolt of lightning, the intent of his words struck her. He was suggesting he would forget her promise in exchange for a romantic relationship with her. He was bargaining with her, trying to bribe her.

She pushed him away, anger rising in her like bile. How could he even think such a thing—assume she would sell her affections in exchange for the broker's commission? She felt she would explode, and her voice rose to a shrill pitch. "How dare you!"

Richard's expression changed into one of disbelief, then shock and anger, mirroring her own feelings. "What do you mean? How dare I what? What are you talking about?"

"You're trying to—" She didn't know what words to use, but she forced herself to continue. "How could you assume that I would pursue a personal relationship with you to avoid a financial obligation!"

"What financial obligation?" Richard countered. Although he towered over her, he looked straight into her eyes.

"Oh, isn't that what this was all about?"

"You mean my kissing you? Don't you think I'm human, with a normal man's feelings?"

"I don't mean that." She sputtered. "You said I didn't have to repay your commissions as I promised."

He stood silent for a moment. A frown creased his forehead, and a spark of understanding seemed to ignite in his thoughts. "You think—you actually think—I would attempt to bribe you into a love affair?"

Her indignation began to wither. Something about the way he asked made it sound as if she doubted he was capable of finding someone who would love him for himself alone.

He turned abruptly, started to walk away, then turned and

faced her again. "Don't be too sure that I'm incapable of finding a woman any other way!" he said in a low growl. "Nor that I think so little of your own standards that I would attempt to win your affections for the price of a Mercedes."

Her mind reeled. But she knew she hadn't misunderstood him. "You said, only a moment ago, that I needn't—"

"I seem to have said too much this evening," he interrupted. "I let myself be carried away and spoke without thinking. But if my careless words gave you the impression that I entertained such crude thoughts, then obviously, we don't have a rapport between us after all." His long legs carried him to the entryway in moments. "Good night."

The door made a small slam as he went out, and Carly's fury mounted. She wanted to have the last word herself. Her thoughts boiled over with insults to his character and his perception of hers. Seconds lengthened into minutes while she rehearsed all the invectives she would have heaped upon him, had he not withdrawn from the battle like a coward.

She ran into her bedroom and yanked off her clothes, all the while remembering every word they'd said. Slowly, rational thinking returned. Embarrassment edged its way inside her mind. She'd obviously leaped to a false conclusion. She'd imagined an insult where none existed. She caught a glimpse of herself in the mirror, her face flushed. She'd been too defensive again. Too impetuous.

She shouldn't have accused him. Still, it was his own fault. He shouldn't have kissed her.

She sank down on the bed. If they weren't careful, the temper that went with their red hair was going to lead to more explosive scenes. She corrected herself. There would be no future scenes. She would never see him again.

இ

Richard plunged down the steps and into the street. "Idiot!"

he berated himself. Why had he created this impasse? Yes, she was beautiful, and he couldn't help wanting to hold her in his arms. But he had never intended her to think he expected to exchange affection for money. The very idea was abhorrent to him. He was not that kind of man. He would never do such a thing to any woman, much less this one, who made him feel caring and protective. There was an aura about her—something pure and wholesome—that reminded him of his sister in Boston and even his aunts. No wonder he had impulsively told them to call her.

But even worse than his possibly destroying any future relationship with Carly, he had jeopardized his mission. At this moment, he wanted to chuck the whole thing, but he'd given his word. Somehow, he had to get back on track and pray he could finish the job without hurting Carly.

Suddenly feeling cold from the fog, which had begun to roll down the hill, he tucked his head down and quickened his pace.

five

After church on Sunday and throughout the remainder of the day, Carly rehearsed how she would approach Richard and what she would say. She had been rude to him. Insulted him. She had accused him of trying to seduce her in exchange for her broker's commission.

The thought of his reaction to her accusations made her face hot even now. His parting words had made it clear he held no such intention. She knew she must apologize to him. Actually, apologizing might prove to be the easy part. After she apologized, somehow she had to let him know, without seeming petty or irresponsible, that she could no longer handle his stock transactions at Wilson, Phelps, and Smith.

After arriving at her office on Monday morning, she went over all of it again in her mind. The steady hum of voices, punctuated by the occasional peal of a telephone bell, went all but unnoticed. She stared unseeing at the wall of her office and idly fingered the edges of *Barron's Weekly* on her desk. She could concentrate on little else but the coming confrontation with the man who had so stirred her that, even now, thinking about him caused an almost unbearable tenseness in her body.

She contemplated a variety of ways she might avoid a confrontation. She considered simply dropping him a note and informing him of her decision to turn over his account to another representative. But that seemed too cowardly.

She could be calm and professional on the telephone. However, her conscience refused that solution too.

Her mind and body were at opposite poles, her brain telling her she must do the right thing, and her body postponing the decision. She rehearsed her speech to him a dozen times. She really must do it now, this very minute.

Soon her phone would ring with orders to execute. She had other clients, after all.

Finally, the choice to pick up the telephone and dial his number won out. She lifted the receiver.

"Good morning." The telephone did not bring the deep resonant voice of Richard Davis to her. Instead, he walked into her office and said the words in person. He deposited himself into the walnut chair, his face a mask that hid feelings she desperately wished to know.

She told the receptionist to hold her calls, then replaced the instrument, never taking her gaze from his face.

Before he spoke again, the frown that creased his forehead disappeared. As if looking at her had somehow dissipated his anger, the muscles around his mouth relaxed. A hint of laughter softened his voice. "No 'good morning' in return? You were much friendlier Saturday night. Well, up to a point."

Carly found her voice at last. "A point you have every right to remember with distaste." She hurried along, anxious to say her speech before she could stop herself. "I'm so terribly sorry for what I said the other night. It was not only wrong, but— I mean, please forgive me."

She let out her breath and dropped her gaze to her desktop.

"I'm touched by your apology," he said, "but I shouldn't have brought up the matter in the first place."

"No, you were right to remind me. Although I was just getting ready to call you when you showed up just now."

"If I were a true gentleman, I wouldn't have been quite so—shall we say 'amorous'—to begin with. You had warned me, after all, that friendship was as far as our relationship was likely to go. I plead guilty to letting the firelight and your beauty get the better of me."

He was apologizing to her. Carly searched his face for some sign he might be teasing her, but he seemed perfectly sincere.

"While I was on my way over here," he went on, "I planned to tell you that I'm taking my business elsewhere. But after a walk in the damp air you people call 'morning mist,' I've changed my mind. What happened Saturday night was entirely my fault, and I take full responsibility." His gaze lingered over her face.

Carly opened her mouth to answer, but he continued.

"I'm used to having my own way, but there's something about you that makes my emotions go all haywire." His voice was intense but not loud. "I have no regrets about *wanting* to kiss you, but I shouldn't have given in to those feelings. Besides, some of the things I said later were out of line. I spoke in the heat of the moment, and I must have hurt you deeply."

Carly managed to cut in. "Please, don't say any more. I don't want to talk about Saturday night. We've each apologized, and so far as I'm concerned, the matter is closed."

Richard grinned, grasped her hand, and squeezed it, but she quickly pulled away.

"You're not the only one to think that it's best if we don't work together any more. I've decided to turn your account over to Ernest Wilson. He's the son of the founder, a fine broker."

There, she'd said it. It hadn't been so hard after all. But her heart still pounded as if it wanted to escape from her chest, and her eyes stung as though she were on the verge of tears. She took a deep breath and tried to regain her composure.

The sounds of the large office surrounding her cubicle suddenly lessened, making the halt in their conversation all the more obvious and uncomfortable. Carly shifted and squirmed in her chair. She looked at her desk, rather than at his face.

He became businesslike again, his voice taking on a brisk tone. "As I've said, I considered that alternative but decided it was not only cowardly, but not in my best financial interests. I don't want anyone else handling my account. I respect your judgment, and I want to continue working with you. For my part, I promise never to make an inappropriate advance toward you again."

Carly's eyes continued to burn, and the butterflies in her stomach swarmed anew. She lifted her gaze to his once more. His expression told her more than he perhaps realized. It must have been difficult for him to make that speech. How much better it would be if they ended the relationship now—before either of them got hurt—but he apparently didn't want to do that.

"Thank you." Her voice dropped. "I appreciate the compliment, but I'm afraid it's impossible for us to continue working together under these circumstances."

"I agree to respect your feelings in the future, but I don't see why we can't continue to be friends. Even perhaps more than friends. We're both unattached. There's no harm in letting things happen as they will."

"You may see it that way. Yet even aside from the ethics of the matter, I have no intention of getting involved with anyone."

"You offered friendship the other night. Isn't that a kind of involvement? Why do you want to withdraw that?"

"I'm afraid I was being naive." She struggled to find words to make him understand. "Look, you know the broker-client relationship is a special one. If the two parties become romantically attached, all kinds of problems can arise. Ethics problems. I could be accused of treating you differently from

other clients, giving you special favors. You could be accused
of pressuring me for privileged information—"

"I would never do that," he insisted.

"And I believe you, but that's not the point. What matters is
the perception of others. Brokers must be above suspicion."

He fell silent, his eyes cloudy.

She reached into her drawer and removed his thin, new-
looking folder. She would hand it over to Ernest Wilson right
now and be done with it. She got to her feet and rounded the
corner of her desk.

He stood and moved to stand in front of her. Her gaze flew
to his face, where she saw his earlier expression had been
replaced by a calm determination. She could see how he usually got his own way. Perhaps she had revealed too much
about her own vulnerability by letting him know she doubted
she could keep their relationship on a friendly basis.

She straightened her shoulders and firmed her mouth. She
was known for getting her way as well, and today would be
the end of their association.

"Don't be hasty," he said. "As long as we're not 'romantically attached,' as you put it, no one can find fault with
friends doing business. We can still work this out."

"I don't think so. You may be willing to continue to run the
risk of further problems—problems that will only end with
pain for one or both of us—but I'm not. I know what I want."

Gently but firmly, he removed the folder from her grip and
placed it on the desk, all the while staring into her face. He
stood inches away from her, and Carly wondered if anyone
else in the office had glanced up and wondered why they
were so close together.

The moment passed. He returned to his chair and sat
down. She did the same, grateful they were no longer in
view. She didn't want a scene.

"The investment I made last week," he began, as if he had found the solution to the problem, "was a very small part of what I intend to bring to your firm." He leaned forward across the desk, "I'm talking about real money, a lot of it."

Carly felt she understood his intentions. Was he really bribing her this time, subtly suggesting she would lose out on huge commissions if she relinquished his account? If so, he was going to fail. It would be nice to see larger commissions, but not at the cost of abandoning common sense. The long hours of Sunday, when she had debated with herself about this man, had ended with the right decision. No amount of money would convince her to continue seeing him and risk stirring that up again.

As much as her temper wanted release, she restrained herself, breathed deeply, and collected her thoughts. "Money has nothing to do with this. You said Saturday night that we had no rapport between us after all, and I agree with you. You can't change my mind by dangling large commissions in front of me."

"You're misjudging me again." His words came slowly, as if he weighed every one of them. "I spoke Saturday night in the heat of anger. I didn't mean what I said. Of course there's a rapport between us. We both know it." He paused. "But I'm not talking about commissions either. I'm speaking of loyalty to your firm, fair play."

Carly frowned. "What does loyalty have to do with this?"

He leaned back in his chair with his elbows on the arms, making a tent of his long fingers. "You offer me Ernest Wilson. I counteroffer with Merrill Lynch."

"Merrill Lynch? What do you mean?" But even before he replied, the answer came into her thoughts. He intended to take his business out of the firm—to a competitor.

"I don't think they'll have any qualms about handling my

account," he said. "Our association could be one of instant rapport." In spite of his words, he looked benign.

Carly slumped in the chair and gnawed at her lower lip. Her thoughts swirled. It had never occurred to her that he would take his business down the street. The stakes just went up. She hated to think what her boss would say if she let such a lucrative account leave the firm. A fiery sensation stole across her cheeks as she imagined how she would explain to Bill Trask the poor way in which she had repaid his confidence in her.

Eyes narrowed, she stared back at Richard and saw a tiny grin turn up the corners of his lips. He knew he had her in a bind. Worse, he seemed to be enjoying it. Trapped, she saw no alternative but to surrender. She turned her head from side to side and signaled *no*. Her words acknowledged her defeat.

"You make it very difficult, Mr. Davis."

"So we're back to Mr. Davis, are we? Well, Ms. Jansen, I can accept that." He leaned forward, his gaze searching her face, his voice soft and cajoling. "I'm not really an enemy, you know. Bill Trask has only the highest praise for your work and my aunts insisted I contact you. I know when I'm well off." He grinned. "And, if you want to be formal, I'll be formal. Whatever is necessary. I won't even come into the office. We'll conduct our business over the phone. Just continue to handle my account. Please."

It was the please that did it. That such a wealthy and power-ful man was almost begging humbled her. Who was she to deny him the opportunity to make up for what he considered his bad behavior? If he was certain he could keep their rela-tionship on a friendly basis, why couldn't she at least try to do the same? Could she work with him again? She thought of the many times she'd had divine protection. Yes, with God's help, she would be the consummate professional with him.

"Very well," she said, straightening her back, "I'll continue to handle your account, at least temporarily." She paused. "But I intend to keep you to your promise. There will be nothing of a personal nature between us, and you will not touch me again. Is that understood?"

"Perfectly."

"All right, then. Let's get down to business."

"Right."

"Just one more thing," Carly added. "There will be no more secrets between us. At the moment, you have me at a disadvantage because I can't let my personal feelings come before the good of the firm. However, I'll change my mind in an instant if I think anything underhanded is going on."

He didn't answer, so she continued. "First of all, I want to know exactly what you do. Your application indicated you work for a newsletter called 'Market Lore.' Do you invest for them?"

He hesitated briefly. "No, I'm a private investor. Recently, I joined the staff of the newsletter put out by Joel Unger, and we're planning to open a branch office here in San Francisco."

The name Joel Unger sounded vaguely familiar to Carly, but just where she had heard it before eluded her. "I'm afraid I haven't heard of your newsletter."

"It's new," Richard explained. "Unger worked in the research department of a bank before he decided to try his hand at publishing. He's only been in business for a year, but he's already making a profit, and his predictions have been remarkably accurate."

"That's impressive," Carly admitted. "I understand that most don't make money for several years. What's the purpose, though, of opening a second office?"

"That was my idea. I thought having an office on the West Coast might be an advantage. Actually, I'm on my own in this venture. I get market recommendations from Unger to pass on to his newsletter clients, but making the office pay for itself will be my responsibility."

"I wish you luck. What about your trades?"

"My trades will not be connected in any way with the newsletter. They will be strictly my own. 'Market Lore' does not trade. It merely gives advice to others."

"I see."

"It's not that it's unethical, or anything, you understand. That's just the way we want it."

"I know it's not unethical. I also know it's relatively easy to start one, but usually difficult to make it pay. Between hiring people for research and advertising to get subscribers—"

"Right. You register with the Securities and Exchange Commission, and if you've never been convicted of a felony and don't handle other people's money, that's all there is to it."

"It really sounds too easy."

Richard smiled and again the attraction to him welled up within her, threatening her composure.

"I agree," he said. "Of course, some people cut overhead by doing it all themselves or with relatives. I suppose you've heard about the newsletter started some years ago by a young man who hawked them on Wall Street for fifty cents each." A broad grin replaced the smile, and Carly could see that he loved telling the tale the way some people enjoyed coming to the punch line of a good joke. "He used an old ditto machine, and his mother collated them on her kitchen table. He was sixteen years old." He paused. "The SEC form didn't ask his age."

Carly couldn't help laughing. "What a wonderful story."

"You know San Francisco stories. I know lots of stories about Wall Street. I'll tell you more some day."

Some day. There it was again, his intimating that they

would spend time together outside of the office, even though they'd just promised to stick strictly to business. Suddenly, she wished they were away from the confines of her cubicle this very moment. She regretted they couldn't be friends. Experience had already proved that her attraction to this man was real. Yet somehow she had to remain professional. She revisited their earlier subject.

"That explains who you are," she said and paused, realizing in actuality, it did no such thing. She still had dozens of other questions she would like to ask about him. "But it doesn't explain the relationship between you and Len Vickers, and why you pretended no interest in Vickers Technology stock, when all the while you and he are apparently good friends."

Once more, Richard leaned back in his chair, stretching his long legs forward. "I'll answer you as truthfully as I can."

"What does that mean?"

He ignored her question and went on. "You made a perfectly valid assessment of Vickers Technology. Their earnings look good, and their stock will rise. But not much longer."

"Is this a market tip from Joel Unger?"

"Yes—and no. The point is, the rise occurred for other reasons. They were the object of a takeover attempt."

Carly's eyes widened, and her thoughts flashed to some of the articles she'd read about the company. "Of course," she began, "any well-managed company can be considered for a takeover. But, in this case, I haven't heard any rumors to that effect. Do you know the interested party?"

"The offer to buy Vickers was withdrawn," he said, not answering her question. "The point is, I knew when that happened, the stock price would drop again."

"But you did buy it."

"You talked me into it. Is that so hard to understand? And your offer was irresistible." He was grinning at her again.

Carly felt uncomfortable, remembering that rash boast of the week before—and her leaping to the conclusion on Saturday night that he wanted to take advantage of it. In the harsh light of day, she now knew she'd been mistaken about his intentions. Still, his own apology indicated he, too, had played a part in their misunderstanding.

"So I'd like to close out my position in the stock," he said. "That will take care of both my ambivalent feelings and the matter of the commission you promised to repay."

She turned to the computer terminal and punched in the symbol of the stock. "Thirty and seven-eighths," she read. "It's higher, so you've made a profit after all."

"And you don't have to give up the commission."

Something about the tone in his voice almost weakened her resolve. If her offer had been irresistible, then what about him, his touch, his kisses? She had to forget those moments in his arms—moments that must never be repeated.

Pushing aside the newspaper on her desk, she filled out the paperwork for the sale of the stock. Suddenly another disturbing thought flooded in. She looked up at Richard again. "How do you know the takeover offer has been withdrawn?"

"I have my sources."

Carly felt annoyance flood over her. He was simply too mysterious! "Did Len Vickers encourage the takeover?"

"Certainly not. Would you want *your* company taken over?" He gazed at her so intently that her annoyance swept away as swiftly as it had come. In its place, she felt a warmth creep up her neck and spread across her cheeks.

She managed to speak in a normal tone. "That all depends, I suppose."

"Well, in Len's case, since he started the business himself, and it bears his name, I can't see how he could be happy at the prospect of someone else having a controlling interest and telling him how to run it."

Carly thought over his words. She could almost hear the pride in Richard's voice as he described his friend's achievement. At the same time, she could imagine the situation from the point of view of someone who felt helpless under circumstances he could not easily change. On one hand, the price of a stock usually rose dramatically on takeover rumors, making the owner and anyone else who held it immeasurably wealthier. With the offer withdrawn, however, the price just as abruptly dropped, leaving everyone with vastly diminished holdings. It was a two-edged sword and could lead to a serious dilemma for a company officer. Depending on the circumstances, this could be considered insider information. And acting on insider information was not only unethical, it was illegal.

"Just where did Joel Unger get the information that Vickers might be a candidate for a takeover?"

"Did I say that it had been Unger?"

"You said 'yes and no' when I asked you."

He seemed to know her thoughts. "If you mean did he have insider information, I'm afraid I can't answer that. All I know is, I didn't have any insider information. By the time items are published in the newsletter, they're already well known."

Warning flags sprang up in Carly's mind. He sounded evasive. "This one wasn't, not to me, at any rate. And I'm hardly uninformed."

Richard paused, his gaze searching her as if for a sign of understanding. "What can I say except, trust me?"

Carly questioned her reaction. This man seemed to always produce such a wide range of emotion in her. Perhaps she had been too suspicious—grasping at straws to keep from succumbing to his charms.

"I think that concludes our business today," she said.

"Unless you want to suggest something else for me to buy." His words were accompanied by a conspiratorial smile that reminded her of her previous recommendation and rash promise. He leaned forward again, his gaze darting over her hair, her face, her throat. A warning flutter began inside, and she wished he would end their interview quickly—before her resolve began to slip. His look alone brought sensations that made a mockery of her determination to ignore the man.

"I'm afraid not," she said. He had asked for her trust, and on an impulse, she decided to give it, but nothing more. Not now.

"Actually, I'm not ready to buy anything more today, but perhaps you'd keep an eye on First Imperial Insurance Company for me. I'd be grateful for your opinion of it."

Carly frowned. Wasn't that the same insurance company whose stock his aunts had asked her to buy for them last week? She started to comment on the coincidence, then remembered the emphasis the ladies had placed on the confidentiality of the account. Again, the mystery that seemed to surround Richard surfaced. She tried to be realistic. He had explained his strange behavior over Vickers and why he had come to San Francisco. As for the stock—what difference did it make that he and his aunts were both interested in the same company? Either he had given them the suggestion, or they had given it to him.

"I'd be glad to," she murmured and again turned to the terminal for the most recent quote. "It's forty-five today. I'm not very knowledgeable about the company, but I'll be glad to check with our research department."

"Fine." Richard picked up his copy of the sell order, and she stood to signal an end to their business for the day. Richard rose, too, and stretched out his hand. Carly shook it briefly and pulled away before she could fully enjoy the warmth of his touch.

His gaze searched her face, as if looking for more than she wanted to show. She remembered his caresses, and the searing heat of that moment in her apartment returned again, driving like a burning poker into the center of her being.

"I'm glad we're friends again, Carly," he said, his voice soft. "And someday. . ."

He didn't finish the sentence but smiled and left.

six

On Sunday morning, Richard struggled to pay attention to the sermon. His thoughts kept wandering to Carly. As he sang the last hymn of the worship service, he pondered the situation again. Never before had he struggled to reconcile his religious principles with the duties of his job. However, his current assignment was throwing a monkey wrench into his personal life. He never intended to seduce her, and he hoped she understood that now.

He turned into the church aisle and walked toward the door. Then he saw her. She must have entered the sanctuary after he did and sat in a back row. His heart thumped in his chest, and he wondered, even though he hadn't specifically prayed to see her, if God might be bringing them together anyway.

❧

Sunday was the last day in the week Carly would have expected to see Richard. As she walked back down the aisle after the church service, admiring the slanting rays of color made by the sun, she suddenly saw him in the crowd moving toward the heavy wooden doors. How had he come to be there?

When she reached the exit, he hurried after her and caught up on the sidewalk in front. "What a nice surprise."

"If you had a feather handy," she said, "you could knock me over with it."

"Same here. I didn't know you attended this church." He glanced back at the tall gothic structure, and she followed his gaze as it flickered over the gray stones and the spidery veins of green ivy.

"Really?" Considering the other times he had turned up when she least expected him, it wasn't too far-fetched to imagine that he'd put his spies to work to discover her place of worship.

"Scout's honor," he said. "But we both live in this area, so I guess it's not that surprising after all."

Perhaps not, but the difficult part was figuring out whether she was happy or sad about it. Her racing heart gave a clue that, once again, she was glad to see him, regardless of whether or not it was prudent.

She turned and began to stroll down the sidewalk. "I thought you were going to buy a condo in Bill Trask's building?"

"Not my type after all. I'm renting an apartment in an old Victorian like yours."

He didn't allow her time to absorb his latest revelation but followed her as she walked to the next corner.

"It's wonderful to see you, and I need your help."

"What kind of help?"

"I need office space, and I'm on my way to check out a place now. Come with me, won't you? I'd like your opinion."

"I doubt that my opinion of an office would be valuable."

"Then come with me just to keep me company. Sundays are such lonely days when you're a stranger in town."

His eyes beseeched her, and she felt herself melting. What had happened to all her resolve to avoid being alone with him? Although she was terribly attracted to him, she knew she mustn't give way to such feelings as long as they did business together. Furthermore, she didn't want a relationship with another man.

On the other hand, however, was the fact that today's sermon had been about being a good neighbor and helping others. All he wanted was a little of her time—in daylight and in public. She was in no danger. She would be downright inconsiderate to refuse.

Ten minutes later, they were boarding a cable car on California Street, and he had changed the subject.

"Why do you have this fixation about money? For a woman in your profession, that seems a contradiction at the very least."

"It is and I don't," Carly protested. They stood on the outside step, and as the cable car reached the cross street and leveled out, she took a firmer handhold before it plunged down the slanting street. "I leave that to some of my clients!"

Richard pulled his right arm free and placed it across her back. She stiffened at his touch before forcing herself to relax. Actually, with the cable car making its swift descent, his hold gave her a feeling of security. A week had passed since their last encounter, and she had become more confident of her ability to remain friends even without the influence of the sermon this morning.

"Maybe you don't realize it," he persisted.

"What are you?" she asked, turning to look into his face. "A psychiatrist? Are you going to analyze me here and now?" Her light tone belied her words.

He laughed softly. "I have only amateur standing, I'm afraid. When Frances and I were engaged, I often sat in the empty theater during her rehearsals and listened to the director, a staunch disciple of the Stanislavsky method, tell the cast members about motivation for their lines."

"Frances must have been good at motivation."

"Apparently so. Sooner than I, she realized she preferred her career to me."

"What has this to do with my so-called fixation about money?" Carly said, bringing him back to the subject. She didn't mind his talking about his former fiancée. She felt no jealousy. She couldn't even entertain such thoughts when she knew her relationship with Richard would—must—remain strictly business.

He paused while the cable car gripman rang the bell. For several seconds, its clang effectively cut off all conversation among passengers. "I meant that I learned a lot in those days about why people react in certain ways. In your case, although you deal in money every day, I suspect you don't really like it."

Carly thought carefully before answering. "I don't like or dislike money, per se. I like what it seems to do for the quality of life." She grinned at him. "Someone once said, 'Money isn't everything, but—' "

" 'It sure beats whatever is in second place,' " Richard finished for her.

"I wasn't quoting that one," Carly said, laughing. "I meant, 'but it makes misery easier to bear.' "

Richard smiled broadly. "I like that too. Say, wait a minute," he added, pretending to be annoyed, "you were supposed to let *me* tell the Wall Street stories, while you told the ones about San Francisco."

"A quotation about money isn't necessarily about Wall Street," she protested. "Everyone knows old jokes like that."

"You're still trying to change the subject."

"Not really. I just meant that money isn't terribly important to me—I can take it or leave it—although I certainly appreciate the fact that a certain amount of it makes my life more comfortable than it might otherwise be." She glanced down at her ice-blue jacket dress. Would she be just as happy if it didn't bear a designer label?

The cable car halted. "Here's our stop," Richard said. He took her elbow and helped her down.

Carly welcomed the conversation's end. Perhaps when it resumed, it would be on a different topic, like the errand they were on today. They skirted the Embarcadero. "I wasn't aware of office space in this area," she commented. "Are you sure they will be open on Sunday?"

"There are some offices available here, but we're going to Sausalito. And, yes, the man I spoke to said he'd be there." They had reached the Ferry Building, and he purchased two tickets on the ferry.

"Sausalito?" She laughed. "Don't you think that's a bit far from the financial district?"

"I've already explained, I like Marin County."

She shrugged. "Well, it's your office. In all honesty, I suppose ferrying to work every day has its attractions."

"I might live over there too," he added, "and since I'll spend most of my time on the telephone, anyway, where I do it isn't all that important."

"Then why not just work out of your home?"

"I don't have a permanent home yet, remember? Besides, a business office should have an address that sounds as if it's in a downtown area."

They waited with scores of other people before boarding. The bay was as blue as the sky, and a breeze put tiny caps of white on the gentle waves and swirled Carly's skirt around her legs. A few puffy white clouds gave a picture-postcard look to the scene, perfected by Richard's handsome appearance.

"Go on," he urged, as they found seats on the upper deck and the boat moved slowly out into the bay. "You were telling me how you felt about money."

"I can't get you off this subject, can I?" Carly sighed slightly, trying to think of something to say that would not be evasive, yet manage to satisfy his curiosity. "I confess I enjoy some of the good things in life, but my parents weren't rich, and I don't know if I could adjust to real wealth." She looked away toward the East Bay hills, letting the cool breeze ruffle her hair. She wondered if he had another motive for his questions.

"But many of your clients must be very wealthy. Doesn't that give you any ideas?"

"Not really." She paused and then something she had not thought of in years came to mind. "I once had a very wealthy uncle—a great-uncle, actually—and when the stock market crashed in 1929, he killed himself."

"A window-jumper," Richard said, then quickly added, "I'm sorry. I didn't mean to sound flip about it."

"That's all right. I never knew him. It happened long before I was born. He didn't jump from a window, though. Actually, those stories were greatly exaggerated. As the Wall Street story expert, you should know that."

"Another myth shot to pieces," he said, pretending dismay. Seriousness returned almost at once. "But you do invest for yourself, don't you, not just for others?"

"Oh, I have some shares of my own, safe things, the kind that widows and orphans are always urged to buy." *Widows.* The word struck her forcibly. She was a widow now. How strange the word sounded as she sat with Richard in the noon sunshine.

He remained quiet, obviously expecting more of an answer from her. As her gaze roamed over the cityscape passing by on their port side, she sorted out her motivations. "Because of my uncle's experience, and the way family members talked about the tragedy, I don't believe in pinning one's hopes and dreams to great wealth. Unlike Uncle Bob, I would never care so much about money that I would die because I lost any. On the other hand, going into the brokerage business was not a carefully thought-out decision. It just sort of happened."

"Because of your husband, you mean. But were you attracted because of his interest in money?"

"I think you're struggling to put Freudian touches into this," Carly said, lightly. "Like most undergraduates at the time, our sole interest in money concerned whether we could persuade our parents to send enough to keep us in movies and hamburgers on Saturday night."

"As I recall, you said Brett majored in business, and then you joined him—instead of pursuing library science."

"You have a good memory," she said, returning her gaze to his suntanned face.

"I remember everything about you." His voice dropped to a whisper. "And I like all of it."

"Don't!" she said, too loudly. She looked away. Perhaps it had been a mistake to agree to this excursion. If he reminded her of the way she had responded to his kiss, she would regret her decision. She tried to change the subject. "We're doing entirely too much talking about me."

"I'm still trying to figure out why you ended up a broker, that's all." He shifted on the bench, stretching his legs.

"I've told you. When Brett was killed, Bill Trask suggested I come into the firm. I went to school for three months and here I am. Although I could never be a fanatic about money, that doesn't mean I can't handle stock transactions efficiently."

Richard paused, looking at her through narrowed eyes, before speaking. "Yes, I agree. I think that answers my question. There's only one more."

"Good! And that is—?"

"Do you ever regret not going back into library science?"

"Not really. Frankly, I think I might have been bored with it. Sometimes things work out better for us accidentally than if we had given them previous thought."

"I disagree. For real happiness, I think we need to define

our goals and then go where they can be fulfilled." One hand went across the back of the bench, and he leaned toward her.

She turned her head away from his penetrating look. "After marrying Brett, my own career in business became my goal. In spite of a degree, though, I started out in public relations at a canning company. Then I worked my way up to executive assistant to a vice president."

"That's impressive."

"Not really. Read *assistant* as *secretary*, and you'll understand. I soon learned it was a dead end." The memory of that bitter realization returned, making her frown and her jaw tighten. "I could never become anything higher or be made an officer of the company." After a slight pause, she let herself relax. The past was over. "So, when Brett was killed and Bill offered me the opportunity to take his place, I jumped at it. I haven't regretted it."

"Since I'm fascinated by the stock market myself, I can certainly understand that, but did you ever think about fighting for your rights at the canning company?" He made a palms-up gesture with his hand. "Perhaps you could have had them up before the EEOC. You seem like a fighter to me."

"Believe me, I tried everything short of that. Yes, they were in violation of the equal opportunity laws, but it would have been a hollow victory at best. I liked the people I worked with. It was the system that needed changing. And if I fought them and won a promotion, I would have had to face a lot of angry people. The job wouldn't have given me pleasure anymore."

His voice turned from earnest to tender. "But it mustn't be pleasant to work in the same place that Brett did, to be reminded of him every day."

He had struck at her very soul, but she didn't flinch. She had accepted that challenge and resolved it. "Strangely, it's a comfort. I wouldn't have thought so at first, but there's a kind of feeling of being close to him. I don't expect you to understand."

"I think I do."

She thrust her hands into her jacket pocket. She felt too fully revealed to this man who remained, in many respects, a total stranger. "Please," she said, "You're examining me like a specimen under a magnifying glass. I came with you today to help you find an office. Let's concentrate on that for awhile."

"I'm sorry. I've overstepped the bounds again, and I have no right to pry into your personal life. But I find people endlessly fascinating. You especially."

"Please don't! I didn't want to continue our—our relationship, but you insisted. So we're going to be just friends, remember?"

"You're right." He stood up and rested the small of his back against the ferry railing at their side. "I'll stick to business for the rest of the day. Just smile at me some more."

His look cajoled, like a small boy asking for a treat, and her stern demeanor melted. A tiny smile pulled at her lips. "All right."

He returned her smile and continued to study her profile, and Carly looked out at the passing scenery.

She wondered why he had asked so many questions about her attitude toward money, almost as if he were investigating her like a bond company. He might be her wealthiest client. Was he hinting she should become interested in him because of that? Or, since she knew a lot about his finances, was he worried she'd like him only for his money? But no. They had already settled that matter. It was *she* who kept insisting they were just friends. And what about his own interest in finance? In spite of his curiosity about her, she wouldn't ask him. She didn't want to know about his personal life, except for what he volunteered. It was a kind of balancing act, making sure he would keep his distance.

She stood up and leaned forward against the railing, watching the wake of the boat ripple outward and the gulls swoop and dive. As the vessel edged into its berth on the Marin County side, he said, "Let's have some lunch first and visit the shops."

"Are you sure you have some offices to inspect over here?" Carly couldn't keep the note of suspicion from her voice.

"One," he said. "I found it in the newspaper classified section. But I'm early for my appointment, so we have some time to kill." With that, he took her arm and helped her down the steps to the main deck, and they stepped onto the wooden gangplank.

They lunched on croissant sandwiches at an outdoor cafe and went into a souvenir shop. Tourist items filled every shelf—trays and glasses with pictures of the Golden Gate Bridge painted on them, plastic place mats, T-shirts, kites, and dozens of knickknacks. They spent little time there, bought nothing, and finally found a taxi to take them to the address of a building that had a vacant office on its second floor.

A quick look, guided by a short, middle-aged Italian who spoke with a heavy accent, convinced Richard the place was unsuitable, and he thanked the man before they hurried out to the sidewalk.

As they stood there for a few minutes, Carly couldn't help teasing. "But you like this side of the bridge, remember?"

"Don't rub it in," he said, feigning displeasure. "I'm willing to admit you were right when you said the city might be a better place to look. Still," he added, smiling down at her, "I enjoyed the ferry ride, didn't you? And you have to admit this town is charming and picturesque."

She smiled. "We agree on that at least." As they strolled back toward the dock, they stopped at an ice cream shop, and

Richard bought them each a waffle cone. They sat on a bench in a nearby park to eat them.

"Would you have dinner with me tonight?" he asked, leaning back comfortably on the bench.

Carly thought for a moment before answering. Something inside her wanted to say yes. She felt very much at ease with him now. Surely the camaraderie could continue without any danger. But almost at once, her imagination pictured the night in her apartment. She felt able, at this moment, to resist any overtures on his part. Still, why take a chance? Why subject herself to more guilt and remorse?

"No," she answered finally, with more regret than she cared to admit. She stood up, brushing crumbs from her skirt. "I don't think that's a good idea. It's getting late. Shall we go?"

He didn't protest but stood up too, and they returned to San Francisco on the next ferry, again on the upper deck. Richard fed the swooping gulls by throwing bits of leftover waffle into the air. Eventually, the birds became bold enough to snatch pieces from his upraised fingers. She grinned. Even birds liked him.

After they docked, he found a taxi, dropped her at her building, and disappeared in the late afternoon traffic.

That evening, she watched a documentary about the sinking of the *Titanic*. She knew she'd done the right thing by refusing to have dinner with Richard. So why did she feel like a passenger on a doomed ocean liner?

seven

While Carly had difficulty keeping Richard out of her thoughts, it was his aunts, the Kemper twins, who called her next. On Wednesday, she lunched with the ladies in the circular tearoom in the rotunda of Neiman Marcus.

"We want to buy some oil stock today," Martha announced after their lunch arrived and the waitress moved out of earshot.

"Oils look very good right now," Mary added. "This new book we just read—"

"—tells all about how to find undervalued stocks," Martha continued.

"—and so when we applied the rules, we found—"

"—several oil companies met the criteria."

"Did you have a particular company in mind?" Carly asked. "Or do you want me to make a list?" She put down her fork and pulled a small pad and pen from her purse in order to make notes.

"No, Dear, that won't be necessary," Martha said. "We've already done that and chosen Standard Oil."

"Do you mean Exxon?" Carly asked.

"Of course. I forgot. Mr. Rockefeller was a friend of our grandfather, you see, and old habits die hard."

"I thought you said you chose it because of a book," Carly asked, returning to the earlier remark.

"Of course we did," Mary said. "But, when you know someone in the business, well—"

"Grandfather would never forgive us," Martha added, "if

we didn't consider someone he was acquainted with—"

Their grandfather was no doubt deceased, and so was Rockefeller, but Carly decided not to try to find logic in the ladies' choices. She simply wrote the name of the stock. "How many shares would you like?"

Mary consulted her sister. "A thousand is enough, don't you think?" The other nodded her gray head vigorously.

Carly's eyes widened as she calculated the possible cost of their latest venture into the market. Exxon was selling at about sixty dollars a share, she believed. The ladies seemed not to bat an eye, however. So she decided neither should she. Carly put the paper away and resumed eating her tuna salad.

"Now, about First Imperial," Martha said, dabbing at her lips with the edge of her napkin. "We want you to sell that—"

"—and sell another thousand shares short," Mary finished.

Carly's hand stopped midway to her mouth, and she set the fork down quickly. If she had been shocked before, she was dumbfounded now. "Sell short?"

"Yes, Dear. We have enough funds in our account."

Carly didn't know which was the more surprising to her— the fact that they seemed to know about short selling or their choice of First Imperial in particular. One moment they seemed like unorthodox neophytes and the next they were sophisticated investors. She pulled out her pad again and wrote quickly, but a nagging feeling persisted that something was not quite right.

"You do know what selling short means?" she asked. "It's a procedure in which you—"

Mary interrupted her. "Of course, Dear. The stock price will drop, and when we cover our short we'll have made a profit."

"That's true," Carly admitted, "provided the stock really goes down."

"Oh, we know it will." Martha settled back in her chair, a satisfied smile streamlining her mouth.

"You did mention getting ideas from a book, but this is very specific—" Carly knew that a correct broker-client relationship required that she warn these elderly ladies about a trade that might not be suitable. "May I ask how you know?"

"That would be telling," Mary said in a sing-song voice, such as one might use to a child, and wagged her finger sideways. "We have our own ideas, too, you know."

"You had me purchase the stock for you only a few weeks ago, and now you want to sell short. You must admit it's puzzling."

"Of course, Dear. But you see," Martha said, "we expect it to go down from now on. We can make money that way too."

How convenient, Carly thought, *if investing were only as simple as that.* "But you must understand," she pressed, "that if the stock price goes up instead, you'll be asked to put up more margin. If you own the shares and they drop, you can never lose more than your original investment, but if you're short and it rises, theoretically—well, the sky's the limit."

"We know all about that," Martha said, a slightly impatient tone in her voice. She sipped her tea again before continuing, "We don't intend to let that happen to us."

"We'll be watching," Mary concluded.

Carly waited, hoping one of them would volunteer further information, but, instead, they changed the subject.

"Mary," Martha said to her sister, "do you have some shopping to do while we're here?"

"Yes, as a matter of fact, I do."

Feeling dismissed, Carly swallowed the last of her iced tea, thanked them, and left the restaurant. Frustration over the position they had placed her in nagged at her. Most other brokers probably wouldn't worry for an instant over the peculiarities of their clients. Maybe she was just too new to the business. Then again, perhaps she had overreacted because she had come to care about the ladies. They were charming and lovable as well as eccentric.

Still, there were complications, at least in Carly's opinion. The Kemper sisters' nephew was also her client, and he had inquired about First Imperial too. Would he also want to sell short? If one client gave information to the other, that would seem to be the next logical step.

Back at her office, she dialed his number and an answering machine took her message. But as soon as she hung up, she regretted her action. The sisters had specifically requested her not to discuss their activities with their nephew. Yet, she had an overriding urge to ask him to explain. Another possible reason for her hasty phone call nagged at her thoughts. Perhaps she had a personal, private need to speak to him, to hear his voice. It was too late to change her mind. She couldn't erase the call. Feeling foolish, she dialed the number again and this time said, "This is Mrs. Jansen. Please ignore my earlier message." Then she tried to bury herself in work so she wouldn't have to wonder what Richard would think about her strange behavior.

She remained in the office later than usual that day, almost expecting him to call back. When he didn't, she told herself it was better that he hadn't, and she went home to prepare her dinner. Later, she collapsed in front of the television set and tried to occupy her mind by watching an old movie. Her gaze fell on the antique tables and bookcases that had once belonged to her grandmother. Her living room, although not as flashy as Bill Trask's, seemed homier, and it suited the converted Victorian house where her apartment comprised the upper floor.

At nine o'clock her doorbell rang. When she inquired who it was, she recognized Richard's voice.

"What are you doing here?" Her face suddenly warmed. Her heart pounded rapidly in her chest.

"I've come in answer to your summons, M'lady." He sounded playful and jolly.

"I didn't summon you."

"Two messages on my machine say differently. You need to talk to me, and I certainly need someone to share my evening snack with. Please," he urged, "I have something special for us."

Her curiosity aroused, as only he seemed capable of doing, she pressed the buzzer that unlocked the downstairs door. Moments later, Richard, with a brown grocery bag in his arms and a very wide, very endearing grin lighting up his face, stood on her threshold. He made a low bow. "Good evening, Fair Lady."

She stood aside and let him enter. "You have a terrible knack of getting your way around me."

"Wonderful knack," he corrected, grinning.

"You can come in for a minute, but you can't stay. I don't need to talk to you. I told you that in the second message."

"All a code naturally, and I, a student of Hercules Poirot, not to mention the San Francisco detective Sam Spade, have deciphered it. You are thirsty, and I am going to make my famous 'Raspberry Davis' for you." With no further invitation, he swept past her and found his way to her kitchen as if he had been there a dozen times instead of once.

She closed her apartment door and followed him, still protesting. "But you can't. It's late and I—"

"You have to get up early. I know. I won't stay long." He took his purchases out of the bag and placed them on her countertop, never looking directly at her, but talking all the while. "You'll love this, I promise. I need an ice cream scoop and a sieve, if you have them."

She found the items while he pulled off his jacket, revealing a short-sleeved polo shirt with some kind of animal embroidered on the pocket. "Where are your glasses?"

Carly pulled out several while he rinsed a box of fruit in her sink. "If I can have fresh raspberries like these every week, I shall never leave California." He placed some of the fruit in the bottom of two of her largest glasses.

"You seem quite at home," she commented from the doorway.

"I could get used to it here." He looked over at her with a smile that did crazy things to Carly's heartbeat. "That doesn't mean you just get to stand there. Here, you scoop the sherbet over the raspberries while I open this bottle."

"So, I get to help?"

"Of course. Oh, and we need some long-handled teaspoons too."

The label on the large bottle read "Cran-Raspberry." Richard poured a large amount of it over the sherbet. More fresh berries were sprinkled on top, and, picking up both glasses, he returned to the living room, where he set them on the coffee table.

Carly followed with the spoons and watched as he dimmed her lights, lit the fireplace, and placed a glass in her hand. He raised his. "To friendship."

She lifted her glass. "I'll drink to that."

"I thought you would." He laughed with her, and she realized again how pleasant it was to spend time with him. She wished she knew more about him.

As quickly as the notion came, she thrust it aside. She couldn't spend time getting to know him. The very idea was dangerous. She must keep their relationship on this light, bantering level.

"It's delicious." She sat on the extreme left side of the sofa and took another sip, then scooped up some of the sherbet with her spoon. It was similar to treats she'd had as a child, but with a tartness that the adult in her appreciated. And it was refreshingly cool. Even so, she suddenly felt warm.

He sat next to her and placed his glass back on the coffee table, then took a long look at her. "What you're wearing is the exact color of the drink."

"Ah, so it is." She held the glass closer to the front of her silk blouse to compare the shade. Suddenly, her hand slipped on the frosty side of the glass and it tilted. Juice splashed forward over the blouse and formed a small pool in her lap.

Carly jumped to her feet, and Richard rose with her. He rushed to take her glass and placed it down on the table. "You're supposed to drink it, you know," he said, "not wear it."

Carly burst into laughter and brushed the raspberries from her skirt into her hand. "Honest, I wasn't trying to send you a message. I really liked it. And I prefer to have my raspberries in me, not on me."

Richard whipped a handkerchief from his pocket and opened it in his palm, then motioned for her to give him the berries she held. When she emptied them onto the handkerchief, he folded it over and used an unsoiled corner to blot the remaining juice from her fingers. As he did, he encircled her wrist with his free hand. His touch sent an electrical charge racing up her arm.

She glanced down at the splotch of red on her skirt. She knew she should go into the other room and change, but her body disobeyed, and she found herself standing still only inches away from him. They stared at each other.

His voice low, he said, "It looks like I broke my promise."

"Your promise?"

"I promised not to touch you, remember?" He relaxed his grasp on her wrist but did not release his hold.

"You were only—"

She didn't finish the sentence. The firelight danced across his face, and his eyes seemed black instead of brown.

"You know I want to kiss you again. What do you think?"

"I think I'd like that, but—"

"But what?"

"You mustn't. I'm sorry."

"My dear Carly." He gave her hand a gentle squeeze, his voice unsteady. "You've done nothing to be sorry for."

"Yes, I have. I've encouraged you and I didn't mean to. Don't you understand?" The words tumbled out almost inaudibly, as if from another person.

"We're not meant to be merely friends. That's what I understand." His breath came in ragged gulps.

"I mean—I don't think I can get over my love for Brett." The words burst from a throat tight with emotion.

He stared at her in silence. A look of intense pain crossed his features, and his mouth set in a tight line, jaw muscles firm and hard. "You still feel connected to him?"

She could only nod, her body beginning to tremble.

She felt him draw a deep, shuddering breath. He let go of her hand and his arms dropped. "I can't fight that," he said simply, quietly.

"I'm sorry," she said again.

He spoke after a long silence, his voice soft and soothing. "I don't mean to come between you and your memories. I want to build new memories with you, but only if you're willing. Only if it doesn't hurt."

Carly saw the compassion written on his features. She realized he knew what it meant to be very hurt.

Tears squeezed from her eyelids. Her shoulders shook.

He took her in his arms again, held her tightly as if comforting her, yet at the same time as if he could never hold her again, then let her go. "Good night."

She looked at the closed door through eyelashes wet with tears. She began to quiver, but whether it was from relief or dismay over his accepting her decision that there could be nothing between them, she didn't know.

❧

Richard found it hard to fall asleep. Visions of Carly swirled in his mind's eye—her silk blouse the color of raspberries, her cloud of bright hair, her lovely face spotted with tears. How he'd wanted to wipe those tears away.

He'd been with beautiful women before, so it wasn't only that her looks were so appealing. After Frances, he'd been soured on women. Then, he'd gone to taking advantage of them, getting revenge as it were. But that, too, had passed. He hadn't been brought up to be either a victim or a bully. He simply immersed himself in work.

Yet now, when he'd finally met someone whom he could admire and respect, she was still mourning for someone else. Worse, his assignment meant he might force her to end up hating him.

eight

The day's issue of *The Wall Street Journal* lay open on Carly's cluttered desk, but she had read the same article three times and remained no closer to understanding it. Richard's face hovered before her, superimposed on the black printing.

A week had passed since the episode in her apartment, but, if anything, she seemed more aware of the man than ever. When dressing every morning, she chose her most attractive outfit. Often during the day, she caught herself looking toward the outer door, expecting him to come in. When she returned to her own apartment and curled up in a chair to read, she found his face and voice intruding on her thoughts and obliterating any attempt at concentration. In spite of having told Richard that she still loved Brett, she couldn't forget the moments in Richard's arms. Since then, Richard's face alone floated before her mind's eye. Even sleep eluded her while she pondered their relationship.

What a remarkable man he was. What patience he had shown. Not many men would have reacted with the grace he showed when she verbally pushed him away. Others might have been angry, called her names, and stormed out. He had been compassionate, understanding. She felt humbled by the revelation. His reaction had been Christlike and compassionate.

Yet, her dilemma persisted. Even if she was beginning to realize that she mustn't let Brett's memory come between her and a future with someone else, she still had the customer-broker relationship to consider. However attracted she was to Richard, a romance between them could never be.

With a sigh, she reached for her cup and realized the coffee was almost stone cold. She rose, left her cubicle, and headed for the break room, padding silently up the carpeted stairs.

As she poured fresh coffee into her mug, Bill Trask entered the room and refilled his own cup.

"Good morning, Carly. I haven't seen much of you lately, but your weekly totals have improved. At this rate, you'll be top rep for the month. Are you out beating the bushes for business, or have your regular customers decided to invest more?"

"Good morning, Bill. I do have two new customers, but mainly I think it's the increased trading of the Kemper sisters." Honesty compelled her to admit where the increase had come from, for, in truth, she felt she had neglected business. Every waking moment seemed to be occupied with thoughts of Richard Davis.

"What are the ladies up to now?"

Carly thought of their Exxon purchase, but more importantly of the short sale in First Imperial. A wave of guilt overtook her. She ought to have been more insistent that they not take such a gamble.

"What's the matter?" Bill asked. "You look worried."

"Oh, it's nothing I can't handle, but sometimes I do worry about my clients. I want all of them to be successful."

"So do we all, my dear, so do we all. But let's be realistic. No one wins all the time, either here or at Las Vegas, and those who say they do are either liars or fools."

"I know that, but—"

"Only one person can buy into a stock at the exact bottom, and only one can sell out at the exact top. And the chances of it being the same person are astronomical. All we can do is hope to go along for a little bit of the ride. If you suggest a stock at a good price, your customer will make some money."

"I believe everything you're saying, but don't we have a responsibility to keep customers from making terrible mistakes?"

"Of course, and I'm sure you try. But sometimes we get clients who seem to enjoy defying us." He frowned. "The worst part is that even though you try to keep them from some folly, which, then, just as you predicted, turns sour, they blame you for it anyway. Then they find another broker, as if he could turn their mistakes into winners."

"I hope that won't happen in this case," Carly said.

He stirred sugar into his cup. "So do I."

Suddenly something else occurred to her. "What do you know about Vickers Technology?"

"Whatever you told me. You did an excellent report on them. So why would I know anything about Vickers that you don't?"

"What about rumors? Have you heard anything of a takeover attempt against them?" She kept her voice even. Impersonal.

His lips pinched, he looked away for a moment, deep in thought. "No— no, nothing of that kind."

"I hadn't heard anything myself, but in the last week or so, I haven't kept such close tabs on them." She considered telling Bill that Richard had confided there had been such an attempt, but changed her mind.

"Well," Bill said, "Harold Yates resigned—he was an officer of the company—but people change jobs every day. Nothing unusual about it that I'm aware of."

For the second time, a name sounded familiar to Carly, but she couldn't recall where she'd heard it before.

"Did you read that in the newspaper?"

"I'm not sure. Probably."

Carly assumed that's where she'd read it too, but if the name of Vickers Technology appeared in the same article, why hadn't she remembered? Thanking Bill for his help, Carly returned to her office. Despite lack of a good reason, she had a sudden urge to look through her client file, and she flipped the Rolodex cards. In the Ys she read the name, *Harold Yates*.

An uneasiness stole through her body, like watching a mystery movie and wondering what would happen next. She pulled open the drawer of her filing cabinet and removed Yates's file. She glanced through it, flipping first to the bottom sheet of paper, his application to open the account. Brett had filled it out, which explained why the name hadn't been instantly familiar.

But the really puzzling thing was that nothing indicated his being an officer at Vickers Technology. Of course, officers weren't necessarily employees. The board of directors could consist of many outsiders. Some individuals did nothing but serve on the boards of directors for various corporations.

Her suspicions momentarily calmed, she scanned the copies of transaction forms. The earliest ones were dated five years before and were for small amounts. Then came a slack period and, finally, about a year ago, a flurry of buy and sell orders for large amounts. Some trades were in Vickers' stock, some not.

A hunch formed in her mind, and she picked up the phone and dialed the offices of Vickers Technology. "May I speak to Mr. Harold Yates, please?"

"I'm sorry," the receptionist answered, "he's no longer employed here."

"I see, but he worked in the—" She let her intuition guide her. "—accounting department, didn't he?"

"Yes. Would you like to speak to anyone else in that department?"

"No, thank you." Carly hung up, certain that an accounting

officer would have firsthand information about financial matters. Would this information lead to something unethical?

But she had no time to decipher what it all meant, as a tall shadow loomed over her, and Richard entered her office. Her heart pounded. The memories of their recent encounter washed over her like a strong tide.

"Richard." She paused for a split second to collect her scattered thoughts, wondering if her common sense could override the personal feelings that almost overwhelmed her.

"Good morning." His smile was bright and open, and his eyes, fringed with thick dark lashes, seemed more hazel than brown. "You look lovely. Green becomes you."

Carly glanced down automatically at her lime-green linen suit. "Thank you." Her voice sounded high and squeaky in her ears. Why must he always have this effect on her? Why did his aura of confidence and masculinity ripple outward and engulf her?

She ignored the symptoms and remembered her phone call. "As a matter of fact, I'm glad you're here."

His entire face seemed to light up. His eyes sparkled; his mouth widened into an even more devastating smile. He reached across the desk toward her hands.

She pulled back reluctantly. "This is strictly business."

His face relaxed and he shrugged. "It's always either strictly business or strictly friendship between us."

She struggled against the vision he evoked—of his holding her, kissing her—but her imagination warred with practicality, and she brought herself back to the subject with difficulty, her face flushed. "I want to talk about Vickers Technology."

"What more is there to say? I closed out my position. End of story." He leaned back in the chair and shifted his legs.

"You told me about a takeover attempt."

His eyes took on a wary look. "It's over now."

"There never was a takeover," she said, her voice low. "There was an insider scandal and Harold Yates resigned." She looked closely at him to see his reaction to her speculation.

His words came slowly. "A resignation isn't all that unusual. And there was no scandal."

"Perhaps not." Again she spoke in a firm quiet tone. "I don't believe there ever was a takeover. I think Yates was passing on insider information. And I think someone paid him handsomely for it. What I want to know is who paid him. You?"

The wariness in his eyes turned to steely hardness. He stared across at her for long moment, then finally seemed to relax again and spoke in low, confidential tones. "I really wasn't free to tell you about it, but I know I can trust you."

"Trust me? Don't involve me in anything illegal!" The thought he might made her temples throb.

"Of course not. I took a very small part in it. Anyway, nothing illegal turned up, and it's all over."

"How small a part?" Her curiosity rose now that the mystery seemed near a solution.

"All right, here's the story. You already know that Vickers is a friend of mine from college days."

"Yes, so you told me."

"Well, he knew I spent a lot of time on Wall Street, so he called me a few months ago about a problem he had."

"What kind of problem?"

"He suspected someone was passing on insider information, and he asked for my help." He shrugged and became silent again.

Carly felt he was playing it down, saying as little as possible. "What could you do from New York? You didn't come to San Francisco until recently."

"That's right. I didn't do much at all, to tell the truth. I told him what kinds of things to look for. And he did. He found out who it was, and the fellow was asked to resign."

Carly thought about that for a moment. "But why did you pretend there had been a takeover attempt?"

"Two reasons. First, Len suspected the information being passed on *would* be used in a takeover. Second, it explained the drop that would probably occur in Vickers' stock. Also, I wasn't at liberty to give all the reasons. Len imposed restrictions on me to that extent. After all, you can't very well catch a thief if you give him plenty of warning that you suspect him."

His explanation seemed logical, but Carly needed still more. "But it's all over now, you said, so why the continued secrecy?"

"Not secrecy, common sense. Yates resigned, but it's not wise to accuse someone. You can be sued for libel, you know."

"But truth is always a defense. If Len Vickers had proof—"

"That's just the point. I don't know exactly what proof he had. Since the press handled it so discreetly, I suspect he didn't have as much as he would have liked."

Everything Richard said made perfect sense. A simple explanation sufficed, after all, and she had been trying to make something mysterious out of it. Relief flooded over her. Only now did she realize she had been almost panic-stricken at the thought that Richard might be involved in something unethical. Strictly business or strictly friendship notwithstanding, she didn't want to think ill of him in even the slightest way. Then she remembered she had seen him at her church. If he truly was a man of faith, he couldn't possibly be mixed up in anything illegal. Tension eased from her body and she smiled.

"At least Len's business is safe again." He paused even longer this time. "Safer than I am."

She searched his face for the answer to that riddle. "What do you mean? You're not in any danger, are you?"

"No, I'm only miserable because of a certain red-haired lady who causes sleepless nights. And, worst of all, who thinks I might have been guilty of paying someone off to get insider information."

Carly felt her face grow hot. She had unjustly accused him—not only that, but accused him of trying to hurt his friend as well. "I'm sorry," she said. "Really, I am. I just discovered the Yates angle this morning and hadn't had a chance to analyze things. It looked as if you were involved somehow, so I just blurted out the first thing that came to my mind. I shouldn't have done that."

"You're forgiven. It was a natural reaction, I suppose. I should have told you the complete story before, although I didn't know you quite as well as I do now." His voice had a low, rich timbre that made her face feel warm. "So I'm partly at fault."

"Don't excuse me completely." She hastened to take her share of the blame for the misunderstanding. "I should have thought before speaking. Sometimes I'm too impetuous."

His gaze swept over her face for some moments before he spoke again. "You're not the only impetuous one. I realize this isn't the time or place, but I want you to know I understand about the other night. Although I can't promise to stop trying to spend time with you." He leaned forward, and she could see tiny strands of silver hair at his temples.

Carly managed to retain control of her feelings, but merely looking at Richard threatened to turn her legs to jelly. "Please don't say anything. I'm sorry about that too."

"You have no reason to be."

"Oh, but I do. And I want you to know how much I appreciate the way you behaved. I—" She stopped, unable to bring herself to discuss her feelings any more. As she searched desperately for a safer topic of conversation, her telephone rang and she handled an order.

When she turned back to Richard, he looked more busi-nesslike. "I shouldn't be taking up so much of your time."

"That's all right." She didn't want to talk about what hap-pened the other night but also didn't want him to leave. "After all, you are a client. That's what I'm here for, to help you with your investments." She reached into her desk and pulled out a sheet of paper. "You asked for more information about First Imperial, and this is from the research department."

He folded it neatly and thrust it into an inside pocket with-out a glance. "Thanks. What's your opinion of the company?"

Carly was dismayed, partly by his seeming indifference to the report she had gleaned from the research department, and partly because of guilt that she had not studied the company personally. Except for some superficial knowledge, she had no information to offer. She had neglected, along with many other things, to study the company because her thoughts seemed dissuaded from work by her musings about this man himself.

"I'm afraid I don't have anything more to add to that re-port," she finished lamely. "Did you want to buy some stock in the company?" She almost added, "or sell," but she decided that would have been too revealing. Did he know his aunts were short-selling it? Should she tell him? Just where did her loyalties lie?

"No, not today."

Again Carly felt disappointed. He had insinuated, boasted actually, that he would be doing a lot of trading—"real money" was the term he used. Yet so far, he'd made only the one transaction, now closed. Her thoughts flew back to their discussion on the way to Sausalito that day. He had been so insistent on finding out her attitude toward money. Now she questioned his. What did it mean to him? If he lost it, would it concern him as deeply as it had her Uncle Bob?

She realized she had missed some of Richard's words. "I'm sorry. What did you say?"

"Not all my funds have been transferred from the East Coast yet. Meantime, thanks for getting the report." He paused. "Any chance of your visiting my new office?" He pulled a new-looking business card from his pocket and handed it to her.

The thought of going with him made her heart jump. "I'd love to." Her voice sounded perfectly normal, but inside she felt as if a trapped butterfly were trying to escape. Then her conscience spoke up. The visit would take her from her job, and she had too much work to do. Although seeing his office could hardly be construed as a romantic encounter, every moment they were alone together seemed to bring dangerous feelings to the surface.

"On second thought, I'd better not." She placed his card on her desk.

"Whatever you say." He looked crestfallen, rose from his chair, and went to her office door. "Maybe some other time."

She said goodbye and watched him cross the lobby and leave the building. She sighed. She was beginning to get very tired of arguing with herself over this man.

nine

"It's Friday. Aren't you going to take off a little early today?" Bill poked his head in Carly's office, suit coat over his arm. Obviously, he was taking his own advice.

"No, I have lots of things to do—paperwork that the boss insists upon." She emphasized the final words but smiled too.

The boss to whom she referred merely shrugged his shoulders. "Suit yourself. Elinor and I are going sailing tomorrow. Want to come along?"

Carly laughed. "And make a crowd? Not on your life."

"Well, if you accept, I'll have to ask a man too—"

"Still matchmaking for me?"

"I can dream, can't I?"

Again the image of Richard sprang, unbidden, into Carly's thoughts and she imagined him on board Bill's sailboat, leaning against the railing, the wind ruffling his thick hair, the bright sun crinkling his eyes, and his mouth smiling in that wonderful way of his.

"Well, what do you think?" Bill continued. "Shall I invite Davis along too?"

"Bill Trask, you are incorrigible. Or else he is. What has he told you?" Annoyance grew in Carly's chest.

"Hold on, there. Richard has told me nothing. But one would have to be blind not to see the way he looks at you. He took you home from my party. He's been in the office several times since then—and always to see you."

"Don't the people in this place have enough work to do to keep them from gossiping about me?"

Bill came fully into her cubicle, settled himself in a chair, and spoke softly. "The whole office will know what's going on if you don't lower your voice."

Carly glared at him for a moment, then relaxed. "I'm sorry. But Richard and I are just friends, nothing more."

"You've been like a little sister to me, Carly. I care what happens to you. Frankly, although I admit I don't know everything about Richard Davis, I think he would be a good thing to happen to you."

"No one's going to 'happen' to me." She had a sudden thought. "Bill, you're the boss. Should you really be trying to push Davis and me together? Wouldn't it be unethical for me to date a client?"

He seemed to think about it for a moment. "Well, if I didn't trust your judgment, I might have a few qualms about it, but not in your case. I'm sure you don't treat him any differently than you would another client. Has he pressured you for special favors?"

"No, in fact, he hasn't bought anything since that first day; there's nothing on the books at all."

"In that case, you really have nothing to worry about. If your conscience bothers you, just tell yourself that he isn't really a client until he places another order."

Carly couldn't keep a smile from finding its way to her face.

Bill noticed. "I guess I solved the problem, and you and he can become more than friends if you like."

"I'm perfectly fine just the way I am. I don't need anyone." Still, she spoke more forcefully than she intended.

"Yes, you do, even though you may not realize it right now. But I have a feeling Richard is willing to wait until then."

"I don't care what Richard is willing to do. It's what I'm willing to do that counts, and I am not going to become involved with him or anyone else." Even as the words were torn from an old speech she had memorized, she knew they didn't represent present reality, and she finished by letting her defiant look dissolve under Bill's concerned scrutiny.

"I'm sorry if I've seemed to intrude in your affairs. Forgive me."

"Oh, Bill, I'm the one who should apologize. I'm reacting like an adolescent. Have a nice weekend."

"You too." He gave her a smile, rose, and walked out.

Carly laid her head on her folded arms and thought about Bill's comments. He seemed pretty convinced she should fall in love with Richard Davis.

The word *love* lingered in her mind. A long time ago, she had heard a definition of love as being "a satisfactory sense of someone." She wondered if she felt that way about Richard—satisfied with him.

Her thoughts turned to his physical appearance. More than satisfactory. There was no doubt at all: He was handsome by anyone's standards. Although she had never put such things at the top of her list of important qualities in a man, good looks were certainly an added bonus. What else? Was she satisfied with his intelligence? That was evident in everything he said and did. What about his emotional qualities? He had proved to be considerate of her, showed loyalty toward his friends, and his engagement had apparently broken up through no fault of his. His aunts, although somewhat eccentric, obviously came from a good family, and he must have inherited some of those same sterling qualities. She couldn't think of anything *not* to like about the man.

"Only Brett," she said in a whisper. And even Brett seemed to become more of a memory and less a part of her life with every passing day.

She sighed and raised her head again, surprised to find that her eyes were moist.

The telephone rang. She had not heard Richard's voice for several days, and its rich deep tone set her heart fluttering like the wings of a moth.

"Carly, I hope you don't have plans for the holiday."

Of course she had none. Until he came along, her social life had been practically nonexistent. Every holiday, not merely the Fourth of July, became her Independence Day. Independence, in this case, meaning lonely.

"Actually—" She spoke slowly, not wanting to sound too eager.

"Good," he continued, taking her answer for granted. "I'm told there's a small town on the peninsula that holds a great festival every year, food, swimming, sailing, even a carnival."

"I've heard of it."

"It sounds like a lot of fun, and we can participate in the sports or just watch. I'm told it's practically the windsurfing capital of the world. Do you know how to wind surf?"

"I did it once a few years ago."

"Great. Then you'll go with me?"

In truth, she had no resistance for anything he might propose. She didn't want to be alone on another holiday. She wanted to be with people. Bill Trask had a girlfriend now, and all her women friends were married. Since Bill himself had said it wasn't unethical for her to go out with Richard, she didn't see why she shouldn't. She needed a day in the sun.

"All right. That does sound nice."

"I'll pick you up at eight tomorrow morning so we'll be in time for the breakfast. Bring a swimsuit and towel and something warm for watching fireworks later. I'll have a blanket for sitting on the grass. It's all settled. See you then."

Carly hung up the phone. So it was all settled? Of course she would go, but her qualms about their relationship were far from settled. Yet was she only fooling herself? She couldn't deny that, since Richard had come along, she had finally begun to have moments of pure joy, happiness with someone other than Brett, yet she wrestled with the idea of loving another man.

※

Carly had lunch with Mary and Martha Kemper that afternoon. Their conversation always surprised her, and she enjoyed their company, although she wondered occasionally why she had become so close to women as old as her grandmother. It had nothing to do with their being related to Richard, either. On that point she felt quite sure. She had come to love them for themselves alone—and their unique personalities.

She spent the first half hour trying to get them to buy back the shares of First Imperial they had borrowed for their short sale. That was a risky business, and to think that these dear old ladies were involved bothered her more than she cared to admit. But they were adamant.

"But, look, my dear," Mary said, protesting, "the stock has gone down. Surely that means—"

"—we were right to sell," Martha finished. "And it's not over yet. It's going to—"

"—go down some more," said Mary.

"It's defying gravity," Carly said gently. "The rest of the market seems to be going up. Look at the averages—"

"Our book says that stocks sometimes make cycles that don't coincide—"

"—with the market as a whole. And this is one of them. You mustn't be concerned. We know—"

"—what we're doing. Sometimes you sound just like our nephew. He thinks—"

"—we don't know what we're doing either, just because we're a little older. But we've been investing since—"

"—before he was born!"

Carly enjoyed hearing them talk about Richard, especially since she hadn't initiated the conversation. It almost felt like eavesdropping, but she didn't care. She regretted only that they hadn't been closer to their nephew, so she could learn even more about him.

"You didn't live near him while he grew up," she prompted.

"No, we had moved out west by that time. Boston is too tame," Martha answered.

"But we kept in touch," Mary added. "We always knew what he did. There weren't a lot of children in our family, but—"

"—we were very close, nonetheless. We always sent him a gift on his birthday—it's the same day as ours, you know—and at Christmas and—"

"—unlike many children, he would write thank you letters and tell us about his activities. We went to his graduation."

"We helped him get his first job."

Carly lifted an eyebrow in surprise. Richard didn't seem the type to need help in anything. "How did that come about?"

"Through a friend of Father's. He needed bright young people to train in his profession, and Richard accepted, but—"

"—just for a little while. Frances made him give it up when he went to New York to be closer to her."

"She's an actress and needed to be where the jobs were," Carly offered.

"Oh, I don't mean that part. She never liked him working for Father's friend."

"What kind of work did he do? Who did he work for?"

"Pinkerton."

"Pinkerton? The detective agency Pinkerton?"

"That's the one. Richard was a detective!" She beamed, as if she wished he were still a detective; or better yet, as if she wished she were one.

ten

On July 4th, Carly and Richard drove down the peninsula in his new red Porsche. His aunts' revelation that he'd been a detective had provided more fuel to the fire of her suspicion that he was far too mysterious. But then she decided it didn't matter. Besides, free from the merciless ringing of her telephone and given privacy never found in her office—as well as neutral ground not afforded by her apartment—she could question him about this new discovery.

As these niggling doubts emerged, she countered them with the need to give him the benefit of the doubt. Her heart would not let her judge him too hastily—without a fair trial, so to speak. If her leaning toward exonerating Richard meant she had begun to care for him, then so be it.

Richard broke into her private musings. "A penny for your thoughts."

"I was thinking in much higher terms, millions of dollars."

He laughed before answering. "I know inflation has been a problem, but I didn't realize thoughts had escalated that much."

"When we went to Sausalito a few weeks ago, you asked me about my attitude toward money. Now it's my turn. What would you do, or not do, for money?"

"Actually, like you, I don't take money very seriously at all." He spoke in a quick, offhand manner.

"That's probably because you've always had it."

"Not so." His face at once became solemn, and his eyes seemed to darken. "My aunts always had a bit of money and—heaven knows how—they parlayed it into a considerable nest-egg. But my side of the family belonged to the great middle class. I had to work my way through college, and it wasn't easy."

"And after that you traveled around Europe—"

"Bummed my way around Europe would be more accurate."

"—staying in youth hostels."

"Yes. Then I met Frances and followed her to New York."

"Hold on a minute. Aren't you leaving out a few years?" She studied his profile while he kept his eyes on the highway before them.

"You didn't say you wanted a play-by-play account, and, frankly, a lot of it was rather dull."

"Not to me."

He turned his eyes to her momentarily to give her a look that said he liked her wanting to know more about him.

"When you came back from Europe, you didn't go to New York at once. How did you live? What job did you have?" She hated herself for this roundabout method of questioning, yet she needed to know if he would tell her the truth. Her heart made a staccato beat while she waited for his reply.

"I worked for a detective agency."

She felt her breath escape and realized she'd been holding it in. She turned her head to glance at the passing scenery for a moment, regaining her calm before continuing. His admittance brought sweet relief, yet she continued to probe. "But you didn't pursue that career in New York."

"No. I'd always had an interest in writing, and since I found myself in the publishing capital of the country, I pounded on some doors. I finally got a very lowly job at *The Wall Street Journal,* and thanks to that, the stock market bug bit me, and here I am." Once more, his tone indicated he considered the subject closed.

"Were you good at it, the detective business, I mean?"

"I guess so. It's not as glamorous as movies lead us to believe. But then writing is not so glamorous either. Why?"

"I'm wondering why you didn't stay with it in New York."

"It would have meant transferring to another office, and I just didn't have sufficient interest."

"So, you didn't ever work as a detective again?"

A frown creased his forehead. "You apparently want to know something else, and I'm not giving you the right answers. Why don't you ask me point blank what you want to know?"

Carly swallowed before saying, "You're not a detective now."

"No." Another pause. "Are you concerned I might be? Is being a detective such a terrible thing in your opinion?"

"Not as long as you don't investigate me." The words tumbled out before she realized how they might sound.

But he laughed. Then he flashed a look of complete admiration over her. "Carly, I don't need a reason to want to be with you. You are far too attractive for that."

She supposed that did explain things, but she still felt the need to know more. Even so, any further questioning could wait for later in the day, should she still feel it was necessary. Now, the bright sun warmed her skin, and as they approached the site of the carnival, the fresh air smelled of popcorn and cotton candy. Crowds of people, colorful tents and umbrellas, the many things to see and do, all claimed her attention. Her mood changed from brooding over his past to enjoying the day.

After their pancake breakfast, served on long tables on a grassy knoll, they strolled behind the recreation center and saw dozens of sailboards dotting the water. The bright Dacron sails, as well as the colorful clothing of everyone on the boardwalk, made a kaleidoscope of greens, reds, blues, and yellows. Wearing their swimsuits underneath their clothes, Carly and Richard stripped off their pants and shirts and found the young man who rented sailboards. Carly chose one with a patriotic red, white, and blue sail, while Richard picked one with black and yellow stripes.

It took Carly several tries and a few tumbles into the water before she regained the knack of keeping her balance. Richard, on other hand, took off from the first and went skimming across the water. When she had again mastered the technique, they took off together and raced downwind. Exhilarated, Carly thrilled as they darted over the blue-green water and passed other sailboards. Half an hour later, the constant motion had exhausted her. She seemed to have a life-or-death hold on the bar, her toes gripped the board, and the taut muscles of her legs throbbed. "Let's go back," she shouted to him.

He nodded, and watching out for other sailboards through the clear plastic insert in the sail, Carly maneuvered back up the lagoon, stepping around the sail each time she tacked. She lost sight of Richard, and when she swirled into the dock, he was nowhere in sight. He joined her just in time to see her misjudge the wind in the cove, luff her sail, and fall into the water.

When she came to the surface, curls dripping, Richard reached down to help her to the boardwalk. "Where were you?" she asked. "I thought you'd beaten me."

"Oh, were we having a race? I stayed behind you all the time, making sure you were okay."

"As you see," she said, laughing at herself. His concern touched her and a deep longing welled up inside her again. How could she not respond to his constant gentlemanly consideration? Like many modern women, she knew she could take care of herself, but she also needed messages of caring and concern.

"You did so well. How did you manage to fall down here?"

"Just lucky I guess." She watched him return both boards to the row of rentals.

"Let's sit on the grass and relax." Richard started to take her hand to lead the way, but Carly shook her hair, sending a spray of water all over his tanned body, and he backed away toward the water's edge.

"You have to remember," she said, "I've had far more exercise than you this morning. You haven't even had to swim a stroke!" With her last sentence, she put her hands on his broad chest and pushed him playfully. But he slipped on the wet boards and hurtled into the water. He came up sputtering.

"Gotcha!" she said, pointing a finger at him.

"I surrender." He slapped the water around him, sending sprays upward. "Is this enough exercise for you?" He lowered his head and swam for several yards, then returned and pulled himself up onto the dock in one smooth, graceful movement, the muscles of his upper arms taut and shiny.

They walked up the grassy hill toward where they'd left their tote bags and clothes. Richard pulled a large green and red plaid blanket out of his and spread it under a nearby tree. "Sit here; I think you've had enough sun for awhile."

Grateful again for his thoughtfulness, Carly felt guilty. "I'm sorry I pushed you. That was childish of me."

"I enjoyed the swim. And anyway," his voice dropped, low and menacing, "I'll get even with you later."

Carly laughed and a comfortable silence settled between them. She let her gaze sweep out over the scene below, barely conscious of the colorful sails and sparkling water, white buildings with yellow awnings and blue tiled roofs that nestled on a small island and, beyond them, the bay and the eastern hills. Finally, she realized he'd been staring at her for some minutes. Her own thoughts, as well as what she imagined he was thinking, made her nervous. It would never do to be so serious this early in the day.

"What are you looking at? Are my ears on straight? I did dress hurriedly this morning," she joked.

"Perfect," he said, "but then, everything about you is so perfect."

She felt warmth rising on her skin. "You do remember, don't you," she said, "that we're just going to be friends?"

"That was your wish, and I'm willing to go along with it, but I can't help my feelings. And I want to be prepared for whenever you change your mind." He smiled and pushed a shock of hair back from his forehead.

Carly thought of the night in her apartment, when she had felt disloyal to Brett's memory and sent Richard away. Since then, he was slowly pushing Brett from her thoughts. Perhaps that was just as well. She couldn't continue to live in the past. She searched Richard's eyes and saw affection written there. Disturbed by the ambivalence of her feelings, she looked away.

The sun shone in an azure canopy of sky that contained not a single cloud. She closed her eyes against its brilliance. After a moment, she felt Richard's hand cover hers where it lay on the blanket. She opened her eyes, pulled her hand free, and turned to look at him again. His body loomed very large next to hers, his broad chest, long arms and legs, sturdy and muscular. The skin was bronze, but as she looked closer, she saw the color was uneven.

"I know how you get so tan," she said. "Your freckles just all run together!"

He laughed and pulled his knees up to his chest. "My secret is out. Now you won't love me anymore, having learned I am not suntanned at all, but merely one king-sized freckle!"

She punched his arm playfully. "You're the largest freckle I've ever seen!" The word "love" had not escaped her notice, but she refused to comment on it. She wanted only light-hearted bantering today.

She jumped up. "My suit's dry now. I think I'll change back into my clothes, and we can look over the exhibits."

"Good idea." He bundled up the blanket and stuffed it into his black nylon bag. "Meet you back here in ten minutes."

Almost fifteen minutes passed by the time Carly had dried herself, put sunscreen on her bare skin, and slipped into her pants and blouse again. Then she added a touch of color to her lips and raked a comb through her disheveled hair. When she emerged from the wooden dressing room kiosk, she saw Richard standing some distance away, talking to another man.

She hesitated, not knowing whether to approach or not, for the man was a stranger, dressed in a dark suit and tie instead of a bathing suit or sports clothing like everyone else in the park. Large, mirrored sunglasses shielded the stranger's eyes from her view.

Richard appeared just as odd. He had already changed back into his tan slacks and green polo shirt, but he held his tote bag tightly under one arm, his other hand apparently inside the bag. From her position, she couldn't see Richard's face, but that of the other man seemed intense, as if he were arguing. Just as she decided to join them after all, the other man began to back away, but Richard stepped even closer to him.

"Hi," she called, moving forward.

Richard spun around. "This gentleman wants to know the way to Gull Avenue, but being a stranger here myself, I haven't been able to help him. Do you know the way?"

The thought of them discussing directions had never entered her mind. "No."

The stranger nodded, walked rapidly up the crest of the hill, and jumped into a black car double-parked at the curb. Carly let Richard take her arm and propel her toward the recreation center, but nagging thoughts disturbed her as they walked. Why didn't the man ask someone else for the information he wanted? Another mystery added itself to all the others about Richard Davis. Every time he explained one, another seemed to take its place.

She couldn't very well say anything. Probably only her vivid imagination turned the stranger's casual question into something sinister. Most likely of all, her fear of falling in love with Richard threw obstacles in her path.

Strolling through the booths of artists and craftspeople surrounding the recreation center, Richard kept one hand lightly under Carly's elbow and guided her through the crowds. As usual, it made her feel comfortable, not patronized.

Besides oils, watercolors, and graphics, there were shell-framed mirrors for sale, stained glass windows and hangings, photographs, hand-crafted jewelry, pottery, and painted weather vanes carved into the shape of ducks. Richard steered her to one particular booth and bought a hand-painted silk scarf, which he draped around Carly's neck and tied into a rakish bow at the side.

"There," he announced, "If I were a knight in a joust, you'd now be my lady fair."

"I think you have it backwards," she said. "Wasn't it the ladies who gave the scarves to the knights?"

"Well, if you're going to be picky about it—" He grinned.

She laughed but then began to wonder if she really did want to be his "lady." Would she ever know? Not if these strange things kept happening. "It's not as easy as that," she told him.

"No harm in trying." He tilted her chin to him. "I do want you to be my lady, you know." The words were hushed, a mere whisper that no one else could hear. She felt her heart respond to him, but she could think of nothing to say, not while her emotions were so ambiguous.

Next they tried the contest booths, hurtling baseballs at bottles that refused to fall down, and pennies into jars that apparently had no openings after all. The games supported various charities whose names were boldly, if poorly, painted on overhead signs, and Richard and Carly giggled and shouted with the many other people doing the same thing. When Richard won a small stuffed bear for her, they were as joyful as if they'd won a cruise.

Clutching her treasure, Carly chose a spot under a tree while Richard headed for the food displays to buy fried chicken, corn on the cob, and garlic French bread for their dinner. She spread the blanket neatly on the grass, then real-ized that in pulling it from the tote bag, something else had tumbled out, a small tape recorder. The turbulence in her middle section returned. Why would he bring a tape recorder to this outing? Before she could give the riddle more consid-eration, he returned, and as if she were somehow guilty, she pushed it back into the bag.

"After we eat, we'll find a good spot to see the fireworks."

Carly put her questions aside temporarily, but later, as they waited at the crest of the hill for the display to begin, she decided to reopen the subject. "So you worked for a detective agency?"

"Very dull stuff."

"But I want to know about it."

Carly said the words quickly, then realized her motives

were painfully obvious. Yet, would she be here with him now if she didn't want to know all about him? He would have to be extremely obtuse—which was emphatically not the case—were he not to suspect her deep interest in him lay behind her probing.

"I went to New York and I got a job writing." Before resuming, he looked up at the darkening sky, as if he could see the past more clearly that way. "As I said, I didn't have much money. My job barely paid the rent, with not much left over. But I spent a lot of my free time in a brokerage office watching the tape—you know, like the people do in your own office."

"The ones in our office all look like retired gentlemen who have nothing better to do. Except during lunch hour," she added.

"Well, I became one of those. It fascinated me. And since I worked there, I read *The Wall Street Journal* from cover to cover every day. Finally, I began to invest some money."

"But if you were poor, how could you do that?"

"My aunts had just sent me a rather large check for my birthday. You see, by coincidence, our birthdays are the same, so they've always remembered me."

"And you them?"

"Naturally. Although in those days, all I could afford to send them was a studio card with some outrageous message on it, like, 'Don't worry if your birthday cake is loaded with preservatives—at your age, you need all the help you can get!' "

Carly's laugh erupted, and the people nearby turned their heads in her direction. She dropped her voice. "They liked it?"

"Loved it! They're the greatest aunts in the world. Everyone should have a set."

"So a crazy sense of humor runs in the family."

"At any rate, instead of something practical, I used their

check to buy shares of a stock I'd been following, and the thing took off about three months later and made me a lot of money."

"Really?"

"Well, not filthy rich, but enough so I knew that's what I wanted to do from then on. It looked so easy."

"You're not going to tell me everything you picked from then on made money?"

"Of course not. I had frequent losers, just the same as everyone else. But I developed a market timing theory."

"Just like—" She'd been about to comment that his aunts were into a market timing theory before she remembered she had been warned not to speak of their investments. "Timing?"

Richard paused and a tiny frown flitted across his forehead before he resumed. "Sort of. Anyway, it seemed to work pretty well, and I quit the newspaper to invest full time."

"Where was Frances all this time? Didn't your success allow you to consider marriage?"

"We'd broken up by then." He said the words in a tight, clipped fashion.

"Oh, I'm sorry."

He sighed. "She dumped me long before my theories began to pay off. She accused me of being afraid of hard work or getting my hands dirty."

"That's a strange accusation."

"Not according to her. Acting is very hard work, you see. Frances knocked on agents' doors, getting occasional work as a model, pounded the pavements day after day, trying, always trying. And she took acting lessons, singing lessons, dancing lessons, anything that might help her to break in. It was exhausting; I admit it."

"It was no reason to berate you for what you were doing."

"Perhaps not, but that's the excuse she gave. She got a small part in an off-Broadway play finally, and frankly, I think one of the men in the cast had a lot to do with the breakup. I suspected they were having an affair."

Carly felt a pounding in her chest, almost as if the pain he must have suffered then transferred itself to her. In a soft voice she asked, "What did you do about it?"

"Nothing. I figured it would blow over about the time the run of the play ended." He lay back, stretched out on the robe.

"And did it?"

His voice was barely audible. "I don't know; she wouldn't return my calls." He paused, his eyes closed. "Later, when I started making money, I kept hoping she might come back. I tried to keep in touch with her—went to her plays. She got more and better parts during the next five years."

"But she didn't come back," Carly filled in. Had Frances done so, Carly would not be with him today, yet she empathized with his agony.

"Actually, she did." Again, Richard paused. He lifted one arm and rested it across his forehead, as if the gesture could hide the painful past. "I had moved to a larger apartment, and one night she turned up, bags in hand. I was so happy I almost cried. She stayed in my spare bedroom about a week."

"I don't understand."

"It turned out I had done well enough to suit her purposes. She wanted money so she could support her current boyfriend, who hadn't as much luck as she, but too much pride to live on her income. Apparently, he didn't have too much pride to live on mine." His voice had not risen in volume but acquired a bitter edge.

Carly sat in silence, unable to think of what to say that would comfort him. She almost regretted starting him on this road into the past, causing him to relive it. She stared down at him and wished she could cradle him in her arms. Kiss away imaginary tears. Comfort him.

Suddenly he shook his head as if to clear his thoughts and sat up straight. "Good grief, whatever made me say all that?" His mood changed abruptly. "I'm sorry, Carly. That happened a very long time ago, and I'm quite over it. I did give her some money, and now she's doing very well as an actress. I'm happy for her, but I have no regrets. No one's immune from making mistakes, and that relationship had been a mistake for both of us."

The sky had darkened; deep blue rose in the east; crimson reds and golden yellows followed the sun as it sank westward. Streetlights across from the park came on, resembling a line of soldiers carrying torches, marching down the street and along the bridges over the winding lagoon. Carly pulled her sweater from her bag and settled it around her shoulders, not answering.

He put his hand over hers as soon as she returned it to the blanket and patted it, as if to say he expected no reply. The fact that he seemed to want to comfort her after his confession instead of seeking consolation from her brought sudden tears to her eyes. Her earlier doubts dissolved into tenderness.

The fireworks began with several small bursts and increased in size and intensity until, half an hour later, they culminated in a grand finale with loud booms and at least a dozen huge displays, colored mostly in reds, whites, and blues. People surged toward their cars, and straggling children lit sparklers, giggling in the darkness.

Carly picked up her things and followed Richard back to the parking lot. No more disquieting thoughts surfaced to mingle with memories of the pleasant day. They were a long time leaving the little town, its one road clogged with traffic, but finally they were at Carly's apartment again, and Richard said good night in her living room.

He took the stuffed bear from her arms and dropped it into the wing chair. She suspected what he planned to do next but didn't stop him. He kissed her gently, his lips brushing hers, teasing. Yet, somehow, she felt as if the fireworks they had seen erupted again, this time in the middle of her body, shooting sparks melting her insides.

At last, her brain took control and reminded her she could crash and burn, just like a Roman candle, leaving—what? Her body tensed, and instantly Richard let her go as though sensing her withdrawal.

His speech was slow, soft, and hoarse. "The time will come, Carly; I know it will. You are my lady." The scarf he had purchased for her still lay loose around her neck, and he pulled it free and placed it instead around the neck of the little stuffed bear. "You keep it," he addressed the bear, "Give it back to her when she's ready."

Then he turned to Carly again. "It's not a leash, Carly. It's not to tie you to me so that you have no freedom. It's only a symbol of a love that might link us together. No matter what we do or where we go, there's a bond between us that can't be broken."

After another brief kiss on the top of her head, he turned and left the apartment. From her wing chair, the stuffed bear smiled foolishly at her, but Carly didn't feel foolish when she kissed it on the tip of its shiny black nose.

&

Not as long as you don't investigate me. As Richard drove to his own apartment, Carly's words haunted him. They indicated, perhaps, that she was still unaware of his actions, but that only meant, in time, her hurt—and his—might be all the greater.

Unless. . . Time. . . He had to get this over and done with soon. She didn't deserve to be hurt, and—with luck—she wouldn't be.

eleven

Carly picked up her telephone and called the Kemper sisters. Since the last time she saw them, she had spent an entire day with their nephew, and although she would have loved to discuss him with his aunts, that was not the purpose of her call.

"This is Mary Kemper."

"It's about your short sale." The papers in the open file on her desk seemed somehow accusing. "I wondered if you were ready to close out your position. The stock has dropped over ten points. . . ." With her free hand, she punched in the symbol of the stock and watched the numbers appear on the screen. "Thirty-and-a-half now, and with the averages continuing to make new highs, I think First Imperial is due for a rebound at any time."

"Thank you for your concern, my dear, but we want to hold our position."

"Are you quite sure? You didn't tell me your objective at the time you made the transaction, but I would think that a twenty-five percent profit would be more than adequate—"

"It's really not time yet. But thank you again."

"Miss Kemper," Carly said more loudly, fearing the lady would break the connection any moment, "as you know, if it goes up, like the rest of the market, and you have to cover at a higher price, you'll lose—"

"Have you heard anything we ought to know, any rumors?"

"Actually, no—" Guilt stilled her tongue and warmed her face. Perhaps she had not investigated the company as thoroughly as she ought.

"Then we'll stay the way we are. By the way, my dear, we'll call you soon for another luncheon meeting. We can discuss it then if you like. So much nicer than on the telephone."

"Miss Kemper, I know I have nothing concrete, but my feelings are strong that you should—" Carly had not heard the click on the other end of the line, but she suddenly became aware of a dead sound. Finally, the dial tone hummed.

"What have you been buying for my aunts?"

Carly whirled around in her chair so quickly she felt her nylons snag on the corner of the desk. "Richard!"

Coatless, Richard's broad shoulders stretched taut against the silky fabric of a pale blue shirt, which he wore open at the throat. He came into the room but didn't sit. Instead, he stood over Carly, a frown creasing his forehead. "What's going on?"

"Nothing's going on." Carly looked down at her desk, instead of into his intense stare. She hadn't heard him come in and she had no way of knowing how much of her conversation he had been privy to. She had been sworn to secrecy by his aunts, but if he heard her last few sentences, he must be aware that she had attempted to give good advice.

"I don't mind losing money myself," he said, "but I hope you're not playing games with the capital of two old women."

"Playing games?" Carly's own defenses soared and she stood up, making herself as tall as possible. "I don't 'play games' with anyone, especially not with your aunts!"

"Then what were the strong feelings you mentioned?"

Carly opened her mouth, but quickly closed it again. His tone of voice intimidated her. She felt wounded. Where was the sweet and tender man of yesterday? She swallowed hard and dropped her voice. "I'm not at liberty to say anything about the transactions of my clients."

"That sounds like a cliché." He sat down, and suddenly his

demeanor changed, and his voice softened. "I'm sorry if I sounded belligerent just now. But I would like to know what stock you've purchased for them and why there's apparently some danger in it."

Carly relished his changed attitude and wished he could be more than just a friend. Still, she couldn't give in to his request. His aunts had made it very clear, more than once, that their transactions were strictly confidential and not even their nephew was to know about them.

She sat down too and looked across the desk at him. "You know I can't betray the broker-client confidence."

"I'd hope my natural concern for my aunts would outweigh any consideration of confidentiality. We're talking family here."

"But you know I can't do that. Why don't you ask them yourself?"

For several seconds, he looked intently into her eyes. Then finally, the tiny frown that creased his forehead disappeared, and he smiled. Her heart leapt. The tightness in her chest dissolved, and she felt herself grin broadly.

He stretched across the desk and captured her hands in his. "Would you have dinner with me tomorrow night?"

"Of course. Is that what you came to see me about? You could have phoned, you know."

"What? And miss a chance to look at the most beautiful stockbroker in San Francisco? Not on your life!" He touched her palm to his lips before dropping her hands. "I may be working late. Would you mind terribly meeting me at my office?"

"Not at all. In fact, I'd like to see your new office."

"You still have my card with the address?"

She nodded.

"Great! See you at six o'clock then."

Before she could agree, he was out the door. She raised the hand he had kissed up to her lips, as if she could still feel his the imprint of his kiss.

Stop this, she told herself. She had assured herself that they could be merely friends, but every time she saw him, a little piece of her armor chipped away. Worse, she had let him kiss her. Encouraged it.

She picked up a pencil and began to doodle on her note-pad. Not silly drawings but words, a list of pros and cons about Richard. *Pro: Handsome, kind, generous, intelligent. Con:* She stopped, unable to think of anything negative to write except one—the mysterious things that kept happening. He hadn't told her he was a Pinkerton detective until she found out from his aunts, but then he admitted it and made it sound quite normal. No sooner were those doubts erased than she found he'd brought a tape recorder to the picnic. And then there was the man who spoke to him in the park.

She should have asked Richard right away but had felt it would be an imposition. If she was trying to keep their relationship strictly business, then she had no right to ask him about his personal life or act as if she suspected him of wrongdoing. If he needed her to know about something, surely he would tell her.

The phone rang, and when the call was over, she tried to push Richard out of her mind. That was easier said than done. Like a spectator at a steadily unfolding drama, she spent the rest of the day, and most of the next, watching the price of First Imperial fall. She went about her work as if a mere automaton, while Richard and his aunts occupied her thoughts.

Then, at last, just minutes before the Exchange closed for the day on Friday, Martha Kemper called to say that they would cover their short to close out their position in First

Imperial. Carly uttered a long, obvious sigh and executed the order in the blink of an eye.

Feeling a burden had been lifted from her shoulders, she felt almost lightheaded all afternoon. At five-thirty, she took a taxi to Richard's office, rode the elevator to the fifth floor, and entered suite number 508.

He sat behind a broad, modern desk of black and chrome, its top totally uncluttered, except for a closed portfolio and the telephone into which he spoke. He got to his feet the moment he saw her and beckoned her to come in, continuing his conversation in a tone that suggested he couldn't wait for it to end.

Carly looked around the office. Two black leather chairs posed neatly in front of the desk, and against the left-hand wall, another chair sat next to a potted plant. In the right corner stood a new, shiny black single file cabinet. There were no papers, books, or anything else in the room.

Within seconds, Richard hung up the phone and came around the corner of his desk. "Carly, I'm so glad you're here." He took her hands in both of his, and at once the pressure of his touch sent shivers through her body.

"I like your office," she said, pulling her hands free and walking past him to the window to look out at the traffic below.

"I didn't expect you to be early. If I'd known—"

"You'd have cleaned up the mess."

He laughed. "Listen, I ought to apologize."

"What for?"

"I'm afraid I was a little short with you yesterday when I heard you on the phone with my aunts. I took your advice and spoke to them, and they informed me in no uncertain terms to mind my own business, which I should have done without being asked."

Carly smiled. "The situation that existed that day, uh, no longer exists. Everything turned out fine."

Richard looked across the desk at her and moved toward her again. "I really knew you wouldn't do anything to hurt them."

She smiled. "I was a little defensive myself that day. I know that's a fault of mine."

"I wouldn't change anything about you." He came still closer and gave an admiring glance at her flower-print dress. "You look lovely, as usual."

She slid away from him, pirouetted as if to show off the fluid silk skirt. His smile told her she'd made a good choice and, furthermore, that he cared for her. A happy satisfaction spread through her body.

He headed for the office door. "We'd better get out of here or they'll lock us in. How about that dinner?"

"Yes, I'm famished."

"But first, there are some phone calls I must make. Would you be an angel and go down to the garage and get my car? It would save some time."

"No, I don't mind. Where is it parked?"

"The lowest level, E, I believe it is." He handed her a set of keys and a ticket stub. "This will handle the fee. As a tenant, I get free parking."

"All right." She hesitated another moment, then slipped the ticket into the side pocket of her dress.

He opened the door for her. "I'll meet you outside in a few minutes."

The slow elevator, as well as her search for his Porsche—which, because of its low-slung design, wasn't easy to spot in the almost-full garage—took more time than she expected. Even so, she waited for him several minutes, parked in a "no stopping" zone, and hoped a policeman wouldn't come by and make her move. She was almost annoyed with Richard when he finally appeared. He opened the driver's door for her to slip out to the other side.

"Sorry to be so long." But he grinned, obviously happy about something and, apparently, not very sorry at all.

Still, the anticipation of spending several hours with him quickly erased her annoyance at having been kept waiting. Besides, she'd been taught to forgive much larger trespasses than that. She relaxed again.

Richard eased the car from the curb and drove expertly through the crowded downtown streets. Then, suddenly, he pulled into a corner parking space. "I'm sorry, Carly, there's just one more thing I have to do." Without waiting for her reply, he unfastened his seat belt, got out of the car, and went inside the drug store on the corner.

Carly assumed he needed to purchase something, but the large plate glass windows showed that he didn't go very far inside the store. Instead, he stopped at the pay phone just inside the door.

That was odd. Hadn't he made all his necessary telephone calls from his office? She didn't speculate about it, but he didn't return immediately. She glanced at her watch. He'd been inside almost five minutes. Again, she reminded herself that she mustn't judge people, mustn't expect them to conform to *her* idea of proper behavior. Hadn't she just reminded herself to forgive another's trespasses? Despite her good intentions, anger and frustration welled up inside. This was different. Mysterious. What was going on? Was it something she should know? Just when she felt so close to him, trusted him, he began his secretive act all over again. Fears, like little mice, gnawed at her insides.

twelve

As Carly and Richard crossed the Golden Gate Bridge and drove north, wisps of gray curled over the red-orange towers. After going through the tunnel, they saw more fog creeping down from the hills and threatening to engulf the highway.

"I love the city," Richard said, taking his eyes from the winding road for a moment to glance at Carly, "but you have to admit the summer is not as warm here as people expect."

"We're just naturally air-conditioned, that's all. But by September and October, the fog doesn't move in from the ocean and chill the air. Even the nights are warm then."

"Good. Actually, there's a lot to be said for a place where you sleep under a blanket every night. I like a cool bedroom."

They left the highway and drove through winding streets—first down, then up. The street became narrower as they ascended and the trees grew thicker, blotting out some of the light. At last they pulled into the driveway of a split-level, redwood-sided house. "Here we are," Richard announced.

"Where? I thought we were going to dinner. This doesn't look like a restaurant to me."

"I call it Chez Davis. I live here." He walked around the car to help her out, but she hadn't moved from her seat.

"You? I thought you lived in an old Victorian in the city."

"I was only renting that. I'm buying this."

Pleasure and disappointment mingled in Carly's mind. On the one hand, it was heartwarming to know that he was going to be a permanent resident of the bay area and not leave her world. Yet, he had purchased the house alone, and, inexplicably, she felt a pang of jealousy that he had done so without sharing the occasion with her. Especially since he'd taken her with him to Sausalito that day to look at a possible office. But again her common sense overrode her emotions. After all, he'd rented his downtown office without so much as a fare-thee-well. Why would he ask her opinion of a house?

"You're very impetuous. Buying a house is a pretty serious investment, not usually done on the spur of the moment."

"I know. It's a habit I find hard to break. Actually, I'm not completely moved in yet. Escrow hasn't closed, but since the building could also be leased, I paid them two months' rent in advance and asked for immediate occupancy."

Carly stepped out of the car onto the sidewalk and followed Richard to the front door. A wide overhang from the roof covered the entrance, sheltering double doors carved from thick redwood. Richard unlocked them and led Carly inside. There was no furniture in the entry or in the spacious living room beyond. Carly noticed the walls were painted oyster white except for one where mahogany panels encased a stone fireplace. Beneath their feet, thick cream-colored carpeting hushed their steps.

Richard took Carly's hand and led her across the room. "Let's see the view before the fog gets any thicker." He pulled open the heavy white drapes, revealing a large, redwood deck and, beyond, a magnificent view of San Francisco Bay, the Bridge, and Angel Island. He slid open the glass doors, and they stepped out.

"This is fantastic," Carly said. "I have friends who have great views of the bay, but this is—well, I'm speechless."

They stood at the railing of the deck for several moments, drinking in the view and inhaling the fresh air, which smelled of the sea and the climbing roses that grew close by.

"It's lovely. I don't wonder you've bought it. Let me see the rest of the house." She turned and stepped back into the living room, then headed right, but Richard caught her hand and led her to a doorway on the left instead.

"Let's start over here," he said. He led her into a dining room, also with a sliding door and view of the bay, but unlike the living room, it contained some furniture.

In the center of the room sat a small, low table of black lacquer, set with white plates, golden yellow napkins, shiny silver, and crystal goblets. Brass candlesticks held tall yellow candles, and on each side of the table rested huge square pillows in the same yellow color with black tassels at the corners.

Carly looked suspiciously at Richard. "What's this all about?"

"Dinner, of course. I did promise you." He strode through an open doorway into a room beyond, still talking. "And, if my guess is correct, dinner is ready."

Carly followed him into a modern kitchen and saw a large insulated hamper on the counter separating the working part of the kitchen from a cozy breakfast nook, again with a grand view of the bridge. He delved into the basket, pulling out covered containers that, judging by his handling, were piping hot.

"Just how did you manage to do all this?" she asked.

"The telephone is a marvelous instrument, did you know that?" He carried one of the dishes into the dining room, talking to her as he went. "I'm afraid I had to neglect you a little this evening while I arranged things. You were marvelous about it, though."

Carly felt a flush creep up her face. She had not been marvelous about it at all. She'd been terribly upset with him for his seeming rudeness, and only her desire to conquer her tendency to be too judgmental, as well as her growing desire to be with him, kept her from speaking out. She was ashamed now of having doubted him. While she fumed, he'd been planning this surprise. How considerate. How thoughtful. How innovative. She thanked God she hadn't said something rash at the time, and she prayed a silent prayer that she'd be more trusting in the future.

"Let me help." She reached for a dish and carried it gingerly back to the dining room, placing it in the center of the table. Three more trips put everything in place.

"Since the table is so low, you might be more comfortable if you slipped out of your shoes," he suggested. After she removed her high-heeled pumps, he led her to one of the cushions; then he went to a small portable radio on the floor in the corner of the room and tuned it to a station playing soft music.

He lit the candles and lifted the covers from the food dishes to reveal bowls of steaming rice; slivers of beef mixed with snow peas, celery, and onion in a savory brown sauce; chicken and almonds; huge prawns ready for dipping in sweet and sour sauce; even squares of pressed duck mixed with vegetables.

"I love Chinese food," Carly said, helping herself to a heaping spoonful of rice. "How did you know?"

"I just hoped you'd like it. We have a lot in common, if you think about it."

"Yes," Carly laughed. "We both like to eat!"

He looked at her across the table, his eyes sweeping over her face. "Be serious."

Carly put a morsel of the pressed duck into her mouth and thought about the word. She understood her own feelings at last, but what were his? How serious was their relationship to him? Was it time for both of them to admit that mere friendship had nothing to do with the way they were beginning to feel?

The flickering light from the candles made shadows on his face, highlighting his nose, accenting his strong chin and cheekbones. His eyes had turned hazel again, with golden tints, as if they caught the light from the candles. A rush of emotion swept over her so that she could hardly swallow. She put down her fork and sipped some of the tea he had poured into tiny cups.

"All right," she said, "but remember you started this. Sometimes you do. . .mysterious things. I want you to explain them all to me. There, is that serious enough for you?"

He took his time before answering. "Actually, I don't think I'm at all mysterious. I was a normal little boy, rode a bicycle at five, learned to swim at six, had a paper route, joined a Boy Scout troop. I mean, we are talking All-American kid here."

"There you go again, always making jokes when I inquire about your past." She took another helping of rice.

"How much further into my past do you want to go? Really, Carly, there are no skeletons rattling in my closet. And turnabout is fair play. What subversive things were you into at the age of five?" After the barest pause, he suddenly said, "What's your earliest memory of the Fourth of July?"

His words conjured up a vision of the most recent, the one spent with him. It had been her best. She forced herself to think back, to one many years ago. "I don't think it's the earliest, but the one I remember is when I was about eight. My family planned to attend an amusement park with my cousin and her family, and after they arrived at our house, Lily suddenly became ill, and my father canceled the excursion."

"How disappointing for you. Couldn't some of you go?"

"My aunt volunteered to stay with Lily, but I wouldn't go without her, so we all stayed home and I read stories to her. That evening she felt better, and we went to the fireworks display. My father let us sit on the roof of the car to watch."

"How sweet. And you an only child. I always thought they were selfish little beasts."

"No. Four of my best friends are only children."

"So single children are unselfish. I'm surprised."

"Well," Carly admitted, remembering one person in particular with whom she'd once worked, "not all of them. But you see, we learn to share because we don't always have a sibling around."

"That doesn't make sense."

"Yes, it does. When you have brothers and sisters at home, there's always someone to play with. But when you're alone, the times with playmates become precious, so you learn to be more considerate and polite with them, to please them."

"Well, I suppose when you put it that way. . ."

"Look at your aunts," Carly added.

"What about my aunts?" His tone was slightly defensive.

"They're lovely ladies; I like them very much. But they have never married. They had each other, you see."

"But they're certainly happy."

"Oh, I'm sure they are. But my point is they were so happy with each other, they never had to make the effort to reach out to other people, to make friends, commitments—"

"Are you ready to make a commitment again, Carly?"

The question came too suddenly; it caught her off guard. She'd been thinking of playmates, sisters, friends—not husbands to whom one committed for life.

She smiled. "Let's change the subject."

Richard poured more tea and pulled out a package of fortune cookies, and Carly broke open her cookie and read the message aloud. "Mine says, 'Good luck is on its way to you.'"

"That's ambiguous enough," Richard answered. "Where's the what and when?"

She shrugged. "I don't believe in luck anyway. What about yours?"

" 'Be brave. Seize the moment.' "

"You're making that up."

"No, I'm not. See for yourself." He held the tiny slip of paper toward her.

She didn't take it. Instead, she picked up her teacup again. "Fortune cookies don't usually say things like that."

He looked at her with a broad grin. "I don't believe in these things either. I'm always looking for the one that says, 'Help! I'm a prisoner in a fortune-cookie factory.' "

She laughed with him. "Anyway, I think dinner is over." She slipped into her shoes, picked up her plate and cup, and got to her feet. "Shall we wash these?" She carried them into the kitchen and set them on the counter.

"Just put them back in the basket. The catering company will do it."

"I must say I approve of the arrangement."

He came behind her then, carrying his own plate and cup. "However, if you really want to get your hands wet, I suppose we ought to rinse them at least." He went to the sink and turned on the faucet. While Carly brought their dishes to him, he filled the single stainless steel bowl with water.

Carly handed him one of the plates, but instead of taking it from her, he continued to look down into the water as if he saw something strange below the surface. At the same time, she felt a movement of the floor beneath her feet. She felt slightly dizzy and wondered if it was something she had eaten.

"That's odd," Richard said. "Look at the water. It was still a moment ago; now it's sloshing from side to side."

Realization came to her and Carly laughed. "Don't you know what's happening? You're in California. We're having a little earthquake!"

thirteen

The "little earthquake" went on and on. Richard took hold of Carly's hand to steady her while everything seemed to tremble around them. Finally, the shaking stopped, and the overhead kitchen light went out.

"Do you always lose electricity during an earthquake?"

"Not always, but that was a big one," she said, "almost a minute, I think."

"It seemed longer."

"I know, they all do. Yet it only took fifteen seconds to topple a freeway several years ago."

"I remember reading about it. You don't suppose that's happened this time, do you?" He opened the sliding doors to the deck and, in spite of the dark, began to inspect the house for signs of damage.

"That depends on the epicenter, although buildings can topple even miles away." She followed him around the property, although having never been there before, she wasn't sure what to look for.

Finally, they returned to the kitchen and Richard did an inside inspection, taking one of the candles from the dining room table. "Everything seems okay."

"Look," Carly said, pointing out through the large window to the view across the Bay. "The fog has lifted a little. I can see the lights of the city."

"It's still there, so I guess nothing much happened."

They stood together silently for a moment, and Carly marveled again at the beauty of the city, the string of lights that paraded along the Bay Bridge, the glow of Coit Tower and the Transamerica building. As usual, it enchanted her.

She turned to Richard. "I guess it's time to go." She returned to the dining room and retrieved her purse.

"I suppose so." He blew out all the candles and joined her at the front door. He helped her into the Porsche, then pulled his car keys out of his pocket, got in beside her, and started the engine.

He drove down the hill slowly, the headlights of the car throwing swaths of light across the dense vegetation surrounding them. Unexpectedly, he slowed the car almost to a stop, and Carly saw people in the road ahead of them. She couldn't imagine what they were doing there at this time of night. Surely they knew it was dangerous to walk in the middle of a dark, winding road.

She peered out of the windshield. "What's going on?"

"I don't know." Richard inched the car ahead until he came abreast of a man and woman hurrying forward. They turned their heads toward the Porsche, and Richard rolled down his window to speak to them. "What's the trouble?"

The man, fortyish, plump, wearing jeans and a heavy jacket, came closer. "It was the earthquake," he said. "Trees fell over, power lines are down."

"Where?"

The man pointed. Carly followed his gaze and the headlights picked up the sight of still more people in the road.

Richard pulled the car off to the side, left the headlights on, and stopped the engine. "Let's have a look."

Carly scrambled out after him and they joined the others walking swiftly down the curving road. When they rounded the next bend, she saw what had caused the problem. Huge trees lay in their path, totally obliterating what lay beyond.

All around them, people were talking loudly, telling one

another how the earthquake had felt to them, what had happened, and why they thought the trees were down.

"They were dead," one man said. "Should have been cleared out long ago."

A woman picked up the story. "The heavy rains we had this past spring must have washed out the hillside around them."

"You got power?" someone asked another person.

"Nope. Lines are down all over."

"What should we do?" Carly asked Richard.

"I don't know. We sure can't drive down the hill with all that in the way."

Carly looked around, wondering where these people had come from. Where were their houses? Between the numerous trees surrounding them and no electricity to light them, they had disappeared as if by magic.

"Are the phones working?" Richard asked a tall man nearby.

"Yeah, someone called 9-1-1 already. They know about it."

Carly shivered in the cold night air. She felt somewhat relieved that the authorities had been notified and soon help would arrive and remove the fallen trees. But what about right now? She looked at Richard again, questioning him with her eyes.

He came close to her and spoke softly, reassuring. "Nothing serious. We just can't drive back down the hill, that's all. They'll probably have it cleared by morning."

Some of the people who had come to see what was going on were beginning to turn around and return to their homes. There was nothing to be done at the moment anyway.

"Is there any other way down? Can I get home tonight?" Carly asked.

"Afraid not. This is the only road."

"You're joking."

"No, I'm not. People deliberately choose to live up here because of its isolation. Farther up the mountain, there are even more houses that have only this one way in or out."

"That seems so. . ." She couldn't think of a word that would describe her feelings. As a city girl, wanting to be at the mercy of a single road seemed incomprehensible to her.

"Of course," Richard was saying, "there's a dirt road— more of a path really—that goes down on the other side. I suppose we could try that."

"Let's."

He helped her inside the car, then made a U-turn, heading back up the hill. After several more twisting turns, the paved road ran out, and they saw a man in a black leather jacket waving at them. Richard stopped the car and rolled down the window.

The tall man held a large flashlight and leaned down to speak to Richard. "You can't get out this way. Sheriff's office told me to put up a road block."

"Are there more trees down?"

"We don't know yet. Thing is, there's an old bridge goes over a stream and the sheriff is afraid it might not be safe. Can't let anyone use it 'til it's checked out." He paused. "Don't want that pretty car of yours dropped into a ditch, do you?" He grinned, as if this were an adventure and he was enjoying his role in it.

Carly leaned over to speak to him. "Is there any other way down? I really need to get back to San Francisco."

"Not tonight, lady. Check back in the morning. Maybe we'll know something then." He straightened up and began dragging sawhorses out of the back of a pickup, blocking entrance to the dirt road.

Richard turned the car around and drove back down the hill.

"Look, at least we have a house to go to." She didn't answer and he continued. "It's not exactly the Ritz-Carlton; actually, it doesn't even have furniture, but we can at least stay out of the cold. I think we can manage just for one night."

Carly didn't answer. What could she say? Staying alone with him overnight hadn't been part of her plans, but there was nothing she could do about it. As they drove back, her imagination pictured the huge dead trees falling on Richard's house instead of the road. They might have been killed. Suddenly, she realized that, in spite of an earthquake, they'd been protected. She silently thanked God and prayed that everyone in the area would be safe and cared for.

Richard opened the front door again and flipped the light switch as if automatically, but nothing happened. "I guess we're still out of power. Good thing we have candles."

As Carly gingerly followed him toward the kitchen—at least there wasn't any furniture for her to bump into in the dark—Richard found the candles they'd used at dinner and lit them.

"The house has three bedrooms, and they have locks on the doors. You'll be perfectly safe in one of them overnight."

She gave him a small smile. "Really, I wasn't afraid. . ." She didn't finish the sentence.

He pulled out two of the cushions they'd sat on and took them into the living room, placing them in front of the fireplace. "I have yet to light this," he commented, "but no time like the present. Lucky the previous owners didn't take these logs with them. I'll sleep here—unless you'd prefer this spot to a bedroom?"

"That's fine. I'll take one of the bedrooms."

Carly followed Richard as he went back into the dining room and picked up the other two saffron-yellow cushions. Then he carried them down the hall to a room that, judging from its size, had to be a master bedroom. "You can cushion the floor with these," he told her, "and I'll get the blanket from the car."

He was gone in an instant and reappeared less than two minutes later with the same red and green plaid blanket they'd used at the park on July Fourth. He draped it over the pillows.

"How fortunate you kept that," Carly said.

"Oh, I always keep a blanket of some kind in the trunk of my car. My grandfather told me how it saved his life once."

"Really?"

"I'll tell you the story, but not in here. If you're not sleepy, why don't you sit in front of the fire with me for a few minutes? We can listen to the radio and see if there's any news."

"That's a good idea." She followed him back to the living room and sat on one of the cushions while he lit some kindling underneath two logs in the grate. "I'll get the radio. It doesn't require electricity, thank goodness."

Twirling the dial, he found only the same music station they'd listened to at dinner. "They'll have some news soon, I'm sure." He sat on the other cushion, and they stared at the flames for a few moments.

"About my grandfather," he said, breaking the silence, " he lived in a very remote area of Massachusetts. One very cold winter, he got his car stuck in a deep snowdrift. He says he'd have frozen to death in the car—I don't think they even had heaters in them in those days—except that he had my grandmother's afghan in the back. It was one of those multi-colored things that ladies used to crochet using leftover yarn from knitting sweaters and mittens for their children."

"He curled up in the afghan?"

"No, he put it under the tires and got enough traction to push the car out of the snowdrift and drive home."

"That was handy."

"Of course, Grandma wasn't too happy when she saw the afghan again—it got a bit chewed up in the process—but—"

"But I'll bet she was glad to have Grandpa home safely."

After a pause, Richard said, a slight tinge of laughter in his voice, "You know, I couldn't have done this better if I'd planned it."

"What do you mean?"

"Well, here we are alone together. You can't get away because of those trees in the road." He raised one hand as if taking an oath. "So help me, I did not plan the earthquake!"

She laughed. "You've already offered me a room with a lock on the door. And I'm going there as soon as we hear some news."

As they waited for the music to end, she glanced about. "You have a lovely house. When did you plan to start living here?"

"Soon, I hope, but it obviously needs furniture and things. A woman's touch. Would you like to help me decorate it?"

"I'd be glad to try." She looked around again. "Obviously, you need a sofa. Perhaps a blue one. Do you like blue?"

"My favorite color."

"And you'll need two easy chairs, perhaps with blue stripes—and some tables. Oh, and Waterford crystal lamps. You can't depend on candles and the fireplace forever."

"Waterford? You like spending my money."

"Well you asked for my advice."

"I wasn't complaining. You can decorate the entire house."

"My, you're easy to please. Actually, you'll need to do a lot of shopping."

"I'm afraid I'm not a person who could do that. You know, someone once told me the real difference between men and women. It's not that men are physically stronger or that women have the babies. The real difference is that women like to shop."

Carly laughed. "Touché."

"Tomorrow you can go with me and choose everything I need to live here in comfort and style."

"Everything? Are you telling me the only furniture you have is that table? Or did the caterer provide that too?"

"No, it's really a coffee table and I bought it, along with a few other necessities, like a few towels and some kitchen utensils. There's a limit to how much a caterer will do, especially on short notice. I only requested a candlelight dinner for two. I hope it met with your approval."

"You know it did. So you're saying we won't go hungry, and that there might be food for breakfast?"

"If you like leftovers. Cold coffee."

"Ugh." She made a face.

"Well, without electricity we can't heat it up. But maybe the power will be back on by morning."

"I hope so."

The song wasn't ended, but the radio announcer cut in abruptly with news of the earthquake. The epicenter had been many miles north and only Marin County had been seriously affected. Trees and power lines were down in many places with homes damaged, but there were no reports of injuries or deaths.

"Thank God," Carly said aloud.

"God had nothing to do with it," Richard responded.

Carly looked over at him. "God had everything to do with it. You go to church. Don't you believe that we're God's beloved children and he protects us?"

"Then why do they call earthquakes and tornadoes 'acts of God?' "

"Some people do—people who don't understand—but that

doesn't make it so."

Richard didn't say any more on the subject, and they both listened to the announcer who continued for several more minutes to report on the earthquake. Then, saying he'd be back with more news later, he returned to music. But Carly didn't stay to hear more. She rose from the cushion. "I'm going to take you up on that private room, but I feel guilty having the only blanket."

"Don't. I'm very warm-blooded. I'll be fine here by the fire. Will you be warm enough?" He got to his feet. "I didn't expect to sleep here for another week, so there's not much in the house. And, since I don't know any of the neighbors—"

"Don't worry about it. I'll be fine." He didn't follow her, and she used her candle to light the way to the bedroom. Not that she thought she needed to, but she turned the little metal lock in the doorknob, arranged the pillows into a bed in a corner of the room, lay down, and pulled the blanket over her. Both the pillows and carpeting underneath were soft, and she felt confident she'd sleep all right.

However, her thoughts were not so easily assuaged. Here she was—forced to spend the night in Richard's house. No going home. No sending him home. She always believed that it was wrong to make love to someone outside of marriage, but she also felt it wasn't wise to tempt fate by putting herself into compromising positions. Now, she felt helpless in the face of forces that seemed bent on doing just that. A further worry nagged at her. Although she was coming to care a great deal for Richard, his comment about God a few minutes ago troubled her. She wanted him to believe in God's goodness as surely as she did. She said a prayer that he would.

fourteen

Although they still had no electricity in the morning, at least the plumbing worked, and Carly was able to shower in the master bath attached to the bedroom, drying herself with one of the new towels Richard had purchased. However, she had to put on the same clothes she'd worn the evening before, including the silk dress and high-heeled pumps.

Cold Chinese food didn't appeal to them, and he suggested they find a restaurant for breakfast before he took her home.

"You mean try to go back down the hill?"

" 'Try' is the operative word here," he said. "Frankly, I'm not optimistic about it. If they can't even get the power turned on yet, I don't see how they could have removed the trees." He shrugged. "But we'll have a shot at it."

His pessimism was justified. The fallen trees still blocked the road. This time there were no people standing about, but something new had been added to the site. A large hand-lettered sign had been nailed to a stake in the ground next to the road. It read, FOOD AND SHELTER AT CHURCH OF FAITH AND LOVE. TWO MILES. An arrow pointed back the way they'd come.

Richard turned the car around. After passing his own house, he drove further up the hill, then found another sign. This one had nothing more than an arrow and the initials CFL. It pointed into a long wide driveway they hadn't seen in the dark the night before. The drive led to a gravel lot with a few cars parked next to a large rustic building. A sign read, CHURCH OF FAITH AND LOVE. He pulled into a parking place, and they both got out of the car. A side door stood open, and as they peered inside, a voice called, "Come in. We have plenty of food and hot coffee."

The room was large, apparently a recreation room attached to the side of the church. Three smiling middle-aged ladies stood behind a long table on which sat two large coffee urns, stacks of Styrofoam cups, sugar, milk, plastic spoons, and four large platters containing home-made muffins, biscuits, and fruit-filled turnovers. About a dozen people stood in front of the table, pouring coffee or tea, helping themselves to the food, while others already sat on folding chairs at some of the round tables scattered throughout the room.

Two young women scurried between the tables and a doorway at the back of the room, which—judging by what Carly could see through an opening cut into the wall—contained a fully-equipped kitchen, where still more women were working.

Richard poured coffee for Carly, handing it to her, and spoke to the closest of the ladies. "Richard Davis," he said, holding out his hand. "I just bought a house down the hill. I didn't know there was a church up here."

"Denise Warshow. Pleased to meet you."

Carly also shook hands with the woman. "I'm Carly Jansen. Apparently, you still have electricity."

"We have a generator, thank goodness." She smiled again, as if emergencies were no big deal. "Help yourselves, folks."

Carly put a muffin and a turnover on a small paper plate and took it, along with her coffee, to the table where Richard held out a chair for her. As they ate, people nearby waved or smiled at them, and still more began to arrive, all talking about the earthquake and its aftermath.

"Didja hear?" one man asked them. "It's much worse farther north. Not just trees down, but houses, a bridge—"

"Not the Golden Gate Bridge?" Richard asked.

Another man laughed, and Carly recognized him as the one they'd seen the night before. "No way is that one gonna come down, no sir. Just a small bridge over a creek. Some roads collapsed too. Lots of people lost their homes."

"That's awful," Carly said. "What will happen to them?"

"Some are gonna come here. We're turning this into a shelter tonight." He paused, stretched out his hand. "Name's Eric Warshow. My wife, Denise, and I are church custodians."

They shook hands with him and Carly thanked them for the coffee and food. "Have you heard when power will be restored or the fallen trees removed?"

"Not yet. This is nothing compared to what's happened up north. Got to wait our turn. Meanwhile, if you folks can donate anything— We'll need more food, blankets, clothes, anything you can spare for the folks that lost their houses—"

"I wish we could," Richard said, "but as I explained to your wife a few minutes ago, I just bought a house here, and I haven't furnished it yet. We don't have a thing to donate. In fact, until we can get back to San Francisco, our only possessions are the clothes we're wearing, four throw pillows and a radio."

Eric Warshow laughed. "Sounds like we need to help you."

"I'd be glad to pay—" Richard began, but Eric stopped him.

"No need for that. We do God's work out of love."

"Then can we at least *help* somehow?" Carly asked. "I'd be glad to help in any way you could use me."

"You'll have to ask Denise, but I think so. Most of us have been up all night and could use a rest if someone can take over."

Richard volunteered too. "I'm ready, willing, and able to do my share."

Eric looked him over. "Not in those clothes. We'll get you some, though. You, too, Ma'am."

He went away, and Carly and Richard finished their breakfast. "Are you sure you want to work for the church?"

"Of course," Richard answered. "Everyone pitches in when there's work to be done. It wouldn't be the first time I dirtied my hands, you know."

Carly was pleased at his answer. Just then, Eric beckoned to him, and Richard got up and followed the other man.

Denise Warshow came up to Carly. "Eric tells me you'd like to help out in the kitchen."

"Wherever I'm needed." She stood up, took the dirty plates and cups to a nearby trash can.

"I've got something I think would fit you, if you don't mind jeans and a T-shirt."

Carly grinned. "My favorite outfit." She followed Denise through a doorway and down a hall to another room. A woman was sorting through clothing while other people arrived, their arms laden with clothes and blankets.

"Here," Denise said, handing the promised garments to Carly. She found a pair of soiled tennis shoes and added them to Carly's pile. "There's a bathroom right across the hall. You can change there, Mrs. Davis. See me in the kitchen when you're ready."

Carly spoke up. "I'm Carly Jansen, remember? Mr. Davis and I are just friends who happened to be together last night."

Denise mumbled, "Sorry," and hurried back in the direction from which they'd come. Carly found the ladies' room and changed into the donated clothing.

She remained in the kitchen all day. The staff changed soon after her arrival, with the newcomers bringing several boxes of food, and luncheon preparations began. She made dozens of sandwiches, mixed up batches of lemonade, and occasionally stirred the huge pot of soup on the industrial-sized stove. She ate her own lunch in less than twenty minutes, sitting on a stool in a corner of the kitchen; then she helped to clean it all away and begin the preparations for a third meal.

At six o'clock, Denise returned and told her to go into the other room to eat. "Your friend is there," she said. "Oh, by the way, PG& E has the power back on again."

"Does that mean the road is open?"

"No, they didn't have to use that road to get things working." She hurried off again.

Richard got up when he saw Carly coming and pulled out a chair. But before she could sit down, he put his arms around her in a strong embrace. "Are you okay?"

The jeans someone had given him were too short, but the plaid shirt, now dirt-stained, seemed to be made for a three hundred pound man. Although he'd washed up before coming in, a black streak remained high on his forehead, and his hair needed a good brushing.

She hugged him back, happy to see him. "I'm fine. You?"

"Tired." He let go of her, and they sat down in front of large plates of beef stew and thick, crusty bread. Two other men sat at their table, and all talked about what they'd been doing all day, searching through destroyed homes for what could be salvaged, shoring up only slightly-damaged buildings, removing debris, checking gas and water lines for leaks, and much more.

"We got more people coming to sleep tonight," one of the men advised. "We'll need to bring some cots in from the storeroom and find more blankets. No rush. Eat your dinner first."

Carly and Richard did just that, then they left each other again to do their separate chores. As it grew dark, some families began to arrive, including small children, clutching dolls or stuffed animals. Carly felt a lump in her throat at the sight of them, and tears welled up in her eyes. She sprang forward to help them fill their dinner plates, then found cots for them to sleep on and handed out blankets.

Just before ten o'clock, Denise Warshow approached her. "It's time you turned in. I saved a cot for you in the kitchen. It'll be quieter there."

"But what about you?"

"Oh, Eric and I took naps this afternoon. You were probably too busy to notice we were gone. We'll take over now."

"Well, all right." Carly looked around, but didn't see Richard anywhere.

"Your friend's out by the car," Denise told her. "Eric said he doesn't have any beds yet, so he gave him a sleeping bag. He could sleep here too, if he wanted," she added, "but since his house is okay, he said he'd go back there."

Carly walked out to the Porsche to say good night, and Richard urged her to climb inside. "Let's talk for a minute before I leave." He got in next to her. "I hear the power is back on. If I had those Waterford crystal lamps you're buying for me, I could do without the candles."

Strange how awkward she suddenly felt with him. Something seemed changed about their relationship, but she didn't know what.

"You worked so hard today; you must be exhausted."

"I'm fine." She reached up to push a strand of hair from his forehead. "You need some sleep yourself; I'm sure you worked harder than I did."

He caught her hand and pressed the palm to his lips. When he looked up at her again, he said, "Do you say your prayers every night?"

"Yes, of course."

"Could I say them with you?"

"Now? Here?" Carly felt butterflies in her stomach. "Does this mean you believe God takes care of us after all?"

"I guess so. At least we were His emissaries today."

She wanted to say more, to really discuss the subject, but this was neither the time nor the place. It had been a long day, spent mainly on her feet, and she felt fatigue in every bone. She bowed her head and folded her hands, and he did the same. She prayed silently for a few moments, her usual prayers, then prayed aloud for the people who had been affected by the earthquake, thanking God for His continued protection and love. Richard said "Amen" with her when she finished and went around to open the car door for her. After she had gotten out, he said good night and drove off.

Almost immediately she missed him. She knew now that she was falling in love with him.

❧

Carly awoke with the same feeling she'd had the night before. She was in love with Richard Davis. No one had ever affected her the way he did. No one seemed so unselfish and considerate, to say nothing of romantic. She had a heightened sense of herself, felt more alive than she had in over a year. As they greeted each other in the church kitchen, she felt awkward and shy, and she wondered if her feelings were somehow etched on her face.

He held her hand for a long moment, then stretched and groaned. "Boy, am I out of shape! I ache in muscles I never knew I had!"

Denise came up to them. "You're not needed at the moment; if you'd like, you can attend the service."

Richard followed her into the church. Sunlight streamed into the sanctuary through the stained glass windows, throwing swaths of color across the walls and over the heads of the worshippers. A feeling of peace settled over Carly. Richard was quiet too, apparently paying close attention to the sermon, which featured, appropriately, the parable of the Good Samaritan.

The rest of the day was a repetition of Saturday. Carly worked in the kitchen and recreation room, preparing food, serving food, hardly ever finding a moment to sit down and rest. Then, in the middle of the afternoon, she supervised children whose parents had gone back to their damaged houses to see what could be salvaged. Richard, too, worked as he had the day before, and that night they again sat in his car for a few minutes before he returned to his house.

"I have some good news and some bad news."

"What's the good news?"

"A crew has been working on removing those trees from the road. They told us it'll be open by morning."

Carly felt her pulse quicken. "Can we get all the way down? What about the bridge that collapsed?"

"That won't hinder us. It was on the other side, across that unpaved road we tried to use on Friday night. I told Eric Warshow I'll take you home tomorrow."

"What's the bad news?"

"I'll take you home tomorrow." He paused. "I don't want to leave. I can't explain it, but these two days have been more meaningful to me than almost anything I've ever done."

Carly felt warm all over. He expressed her sentiments exactly.

"I used to think the stock market was a thrill—you know, making decisions and seeing them work out. But this weekend. . .helping other people. . .feeling really *needed*. . . doing something important. . . Well, it makes everything else seem shallow by comparison. Sure, I've always gone to church, and I've tried to live by the Ten Commandments, but now I feel, well—committed."

"I'm glad."

"There's something else." He paused. "I know that part of what I'm feeling is because you were there doing it with me."

"Not exactly together. You worked outside the church, and I worked inside. We hardly exchanged two sentences."

"But we were helping people who needed us, each in our own way. I loved that, and I'm glad we did, but I have needs too, you know. One of them is to spend more time with you."

Carly turned her head away, trying to sort out her own needs. She wanted to spend her whole life with him. He was, somehow, larger than life, tall, handsome, strong, and yet tender and compassionate. And now—

When she didn't answer, he said, "I'm serious about wanting you to help me decorate my house. If the earthquake hadn't happened, I was going to take you shopping with me this weekend and let you choose everything. And we can still do that."

"You're very impetuous, buying a house so quickly. I don't want to think you're that way about the people in your life."

"There's no reason to think that, because it isn't true." His eyes held her gaze. "Even when I buy things on impulse, I don't necessarily have a lower opinion of those things or tire of them more quickly than the purchases I've pondered a long time over. And, as for you, I've known you a month—thirty-nine days to be exact—but it seems more like forever. I'm in love with you, Carly."

He loves me! She felt her throat tighten, and sudden tears sprang to her eyes.

He took her hands in his and looked at her intently, as if waiting for her reply. But she couldn't speak. Visions of Richard whirled around in her head—the effortless way he did things, his infectious laugh, the warmth of his endearing smile. Still, she couldn't speak.

"Okay," he said in a dejected tone. "I guess you need to think about that for awhile. Not that it should come as any surprise to you. You ought to know I've loved you almost since the moment I first saw you." He hurried on. "But meanwhile, can't you spend some time with me for the next few days?"

"I have a job, remember?" She couldn't imagine where those had words came from. She loved her job, but now it dwindled into insignificance. She felt as if she and Richard were joined in spirit, forged in a bond that was stronger than anything she'd ever known before.

Finally, she blurted out the words. "I love you, too."

fifteen

Carly lay awake for hours, remembering everything she and Richard had done for the past three days, especially those few minutes in his car when she told him she loved him.

He hadn't spoken for a moment. "Say that again."

She repeated it, her voice sounding strange, trembling.

He had swept her into his arms, kissed her passionately, then suddenly turned very businesslike. "We have so much to talk about," he'd said, "plans to make." Finally, saying he'd pick her up at the church early the next morning, he had kissed her again and drove off while she went inside the church to her cot. But it was daylight before she fell into a deep sleep. Sounds of people arriving in the kitchen woke her at last, and she put her cot away, then washed quickly, aware that other people needed to use the building's few restrooms. She put on her silk dress again, returning the clothes she'd been given.

Denise hugged her as if they'd known each other for years. "Thanks so much for helping out."

"I wish I could stay longer, but—"

"I understand. You have a job to go to. Is Richard waiting for you now?"

"I don't know. Perhaps I'd better look outside."

Denise walked to the door with her, and at that moment, Eric Warshow came in. He, too, hugged Carly and thanked her. They said their good-byes, assuring one another they'd meet again.

As they stepped out onto the gravel driveway in front of the building, Eric said, "I don't see your friend's car. You want a lift down to Richard's house?"

"Oh, that won't be necessary."

"No trouble at all. I have to go right past it. Now that the road's open, I've got to go down and get supplies."

"Well, if you don't mind—" She didn't know what was keeping Richard, but the sooner they were on their way, the better. Normally, on a Monday morning, she would have been at her office a good two hours ago.

"Hop in." Eric held open the door of a well-used green pickup truck, and Carly climbed into the passenger seat.

Less than five minutes later, he dropped her off next to the red Porsche parked at the door of "Chez Davis," as Richard had jokingly referred to his new home. She waved good-bye to Eric, and after he drove away, she went up the two shallow steps to the front door. It was not only unlocked, it was standing slightly ajar, as if he'd been on his way out, but had suddenly changed his mind and gone back inside for something.

"Richard?" She called but got no answer. She crossed the living room. The smell of fresh brewed coffee drew her toward the kitchen, and she padded over the dining room carpet soundlessly. Richard spoke to someone on the telephone, his back to her. His head was tilted down, his shoulders hunched.

He obviously had not heard her come in, but she could hear his side of the conversation.

"No one told me they'd do that this morning. But I think I should have been informed—I assume the tapes arrived— Yes, the investigation proceeded very smoothly, better than I thought. Mrs. Jansen doesn't know—"

Carly stood in the kitchen doorway, heart pounding, throat tight. His words rang in her head. *The investigation went smoothly. . . Mrs. Jansen doesn't know. . .*

She felt sick.

"Okay," Richard said. "Talk to you later." He hung up and stood still, staring at the telephone as if deep in thought.

She stepped onto the tiled kitchen floor, her heels clicking.

He whirled around. Surprise and dismay showed in his face. "Carly!"

For a moment, she couldn't speak; she thought her heart would explode. Finally, words formed. "You—you—" She stood still, felt her fists clench at her sides, her breath beginning to come in short gasps. "I trusted you, and you—"

"Carly, what did you hear?"

"I heard it all! You've been investigating me! Time after time, I had suspicions and you always managed to lie—"

"I never lied to you." He moved toward her, but she stopped him with a look.

"First came the mysterious business about Len Vickers—but you had an answer for that. And the man in the park—you said he asked you for directions, but you knew him, didn't you? Who was he? Another spy? Was he following me, too, just in case you missed something?"

She knew her voice rose and became shrill, but she didn't care. She wanted to do more than shout. She wanted to scream. To throw things at him. To claw at his face with her nails. How dare he do this to her!

"Carly, you're not listening to me."

"Oh, I listened to you before. Last night you said you loved me, and like a fool, I believed you—when all the time you were spying on me!"

"No—"

"You pretended to care for me, but instead you were only investigating." The last words were almost a shriek.

"Carly, you must calm down and let me explain."

Her face burning, she realized she could hardly breathe. "Go ahead, start explaining again. That ought to be a laugh!"

"First I have to call New York again. I'm not even sure I can tell you anything."

"Oh, that's a good one," she said sarcastically. "That's very good."

"You have to believe me; I would never hurt you."

"Just answer one question. The truth, Richard. Make it the truth just this once."

"Anything."

"Were you investigating me?"

His eyes bore into hers, and the golden brown color seemed to change to deep black. Pain etched lines down his cheeks and set his jaw into a hard ridge. Seconds passed before the muffled word finally emerged. "Yes."

Carly thought she would faint. He could have lied, but instead he told the truth. At this moment, that was even harder to bear. She forced the words from her throat. "That's all I need to hear."

She turned and left the kitchen, but he followed and stopped her when she got to the front hallway.

"But it's not what you think," he said. "I did investigate you. I had to. But later, I realized you weren't involved."

"You pretended. It was all an act."

"I never acted with you, Carly. I fell in love with you right from the start. I love you now."

"Lying comes easily to you. That's part of your job, isn't it? You're a detective."

"I used to be."

"And then you quit when you went to New York. Don't bother telling me that lie again. I remember it from before."

Suddenly the doorbell rang, its chimes echoed loudly against the empty walls. Richard gave her a pleading look, then he crossed to the front door and opened it. A uniformed man stood there. Carly could see his truck, "Bay Area

Catering," parked at the curb.

"I'm here for a pick-up," the young man said. "Hey, you guys had some earthquake, didn't you? I was surprised I could even get up here today."

Richard cut him short. "The containers are in the kitchen."

The young man shrugged and came inside.

"Are you going back to the city?" Carly asked, her thoughts racing. "Will you take me with you?"

He looked puzzled, seemed about to say "no," then apparently changed his mind. "Sure, Lady, I can drop you downtown." He went into the kitchen and retrieved the containers.

Carly ran out the door and toward his truck.

Richard came up behind her, his voice tense, pleading. "Carly, don't do this to us. I can explain. Believe me. I just need a little time. I'm not in this alone, you know. I have to obey orders."

"I have nothing to say to you, and there's nothing you could possibly say to me." Amazingly, her voice sounded calm, but her heart felt as if it were being torn in two.

Her eyes burned with unshed tears, but after she climbed into the seat next to the driver, and he pulled away down the hill, she let them come. They ran down her face silently, making salty pools at the corners of her mouth.

sixteen

Carly rode back to the city under a dazzlingly bright sun. For once, the sight held no pleasure for her. Instead, her tears flowed faster. The mood established over the weekend was broken. They had said they loved each other, but now the reality of his mysterious past and his confession had plunged her into depths of pain and despair that no amount of sunshine could reach.

The driver of the catering truck respected her mood and didn't speak. Finally, she dried her tears. "Thanks for the lift. Sorry about my behavior, but it's been a rough morning."

"I understand," he said. "Like the song says, breaking up is hard to do." After a pause, he added, "You want some coffee? I got some in that thermos, and there's cups in the plastic bag."

Carly picked up the thermos, unscrewed the top, and poured coffee into one of the Styrofoam cups. Trying to strike up a conversation, she forced herself to talk about the earthquake.

"It was a six-point-seven," he said, "pretty strong."

"Yes, some houses were damaged and trees uprooted." She told him how the trees in the road had prevented them from leaving the area and how the local church had helped everyone, without mentioning her own role in the process.

He dropped her off at her apartment, where she paused only long enough to take a proper shower and change into a clean suit; then she hopped into a cable car to her office. She threw her purse into a drawer and unfolded *The Wall Street*

154

Journal, which lay on her desk.

On page one, an article about First Imperial leapt out at her. After the stock dropped another five points on Friday, the Securities and Exchange Commission considered investigating irregularities in trading, suspecting insider manipulation. She read on, her pulse steadily mounting, as she tried to sort out what it meant to her and to her clients. Almost automatically, she punched the keys of the terminal to get a quote, and the words TRADING SUSPENDED flashed at her. No one could buy or sell shares in the stock until the ban was lifted.

Her thoughts flew to Richard's aunts, the Kemper sisters. They'd been selling the stock short and had covered on Friday, making a very tidy profit. The move seemed too lucky. Too convenient. Carly suspected they had gotten insider information. Richard's face floated before her eyes. Of course. He gave it to them.

First, there had been Vickers Technology. He had known the takeover attempt wouldn't succeed, but he couldn't have known that, unless he had access to illegal information. She'd asked him these questions before, and he covered by saying it was not really a takeover but someone selling confidential information. Now, her doubts returned stronger than ever. Perhaps Len Vickers himself had given information to Richard. They'd been college friends, after all, and although Richard told her he had never been to San Francisco until then, that didn't make it true. Men lied to women all the time—even women they said they cared for deeply.

The churning in her stomach became unbearable, and Carly rested her face in the palms of her hands. She loved Richard. At least she'd been certain of that last night. But his revelation made it clear he was involved in something illegal.

The only one she knew to turn to for advice was Bill Trask.

She would ask him.

At once she rejected the idea. In the first place, it would be too humiliating to admit that the man in her life might be some kind of criminal. Second, she had no proof of anything. She had overheard a telephone conversation and had accused him of spying on her, which he admitted. Nothing more. Perhaps she should have stayed. Questioned him. Gotten the facts. But his betrayal drove everything else from her head. She could hardly bear to think that, after finally allowing herself to love again, she'd chosen a man who now brought her nothing but pain and anguish.

Her telephone rang. Pushing her thoughts aside, she took the call. When she finished answering her client's questions, she turned again to her dilemma over Richard.

She decided to call Joel Unger, the owner of the newsletter Richard worked for, *Market Lore*. She would find out from Mr. Unger just how much he knew about Richard Davis. But no one answered the telephone when she called the number Richard had given her.

A deep voice greeted her. "Carly." Richard came into her cubicle and dropped into the opposite chair.

Shock made her knees weak and her stomach tight. "How dare you come here?" she said between clenched teeth, fighting to keep her voice low.

"I need to talk to you." He wore a tan business suit, shirt and tie, and he looked as handsome as ever, although pale.

"About what?" she hissed. "Surely it couldn't be about First Imperial stock?"

"Then you've heard?"

"I'm probably the last broker in San Francisco to have learned it, but, yes, I heard."

"I'll explain everything if you'll just listen."

"About your involvement? You are involved in it, aren't

you? Or is it about your aunts' selling, about your passing insider information to them?"

"My aunts' selling? What do you mean?"

"I mean they were short-selling the stock. Don't pretend you didn't know. Obviously, you put them up to it. They closed out their position Friday." She almost shouted the last word. "How else could they know this would happen?"

"They were short-selling? This is ridiculous!"

"I wasn't to tell you," Carly said. "They swore me to secrecy. What a fool I've been!"

"Carly, please believe me when I say I knew nothing about that. When I questioned you about your recommendations to my aunts and you told me to ask them, I did just that. But they refused to tell me. I had no idea they were involved in this."

"How can I believe anything you say? You were spying on me, telling me you loved me to keep me from suspecting the truth." Saying the words aloud brought fresh bursts of pain, and she closed her eyes tightly.

"Just what do you think the truth is? What do you hold me responsible for?"

Carly had been unable to answer that question herself. In some ways, nothing made sense. Slowly, she voiced her fears. Her voice softened. "You had insider information about First Imperial, and you passed it on to a lot of people, not just your aunts."

"Why would I do that?"

"For money, of course."

"That's not so."

"There's still Vickers Technology."

"I've already explained that."

"First you said there was to be a takeover, then you changed it to insider fraud, and now the same thing is happening at First Imperial. And you were involved in both of them." He couldn't deny it in the face of all the evidence.

Before he could answer, her telephone rang, and Carly picked it up. She listened, made notes, and finally hung up.

"Wait a minute," Richard said. "I can clear up everything if you'll just let me explain."

Again the telephone interrupted them, and Carly handled the call without a glance toward Richard.

"Carly, you can't have it both ways. If I had all this insider information, why would I need to spy on you? You certainly didn't pass any on to me."

"You wanted to be sure I hadn't caught on—"

His bitter laugh interrupted her. "I should have told you at the time, but I couldn't take a chance. I have no reason to reproach myself, unless it's because of falling in love with you."

Carly's heart plummeted. Did he regret everything he'd said? But, surely, she'd played the bigger fool for having allowed herself to do the same, when she knew so little about him. Now he pretended to be the victim. Her anger flared. "Since you're used to lying, I'm sure you can clear your conscience."

His face changed. Lines creased his forehead and appeared at the corners of his mouth. "Apparently, our weekend together didn't mean as much to you as it did to me."

"I think that's obvious. I thought we were learning to care for each other. Instead, you used me. I was never anything more to you than a 'case.' "

The telephone jangled at her side.

Richard exploded. "I'd stand a better chance of talking to you if I went to a phone booth! I certainly can't do it here. I'll come by your apartment tonight and explain it all."

"I don't recall inviting you to my apartment." Her hurt made her eyes burn and her vision blur.

He'd been on his feet for several seconds, and now he

leaned forward across the desk and stared into her eyes. "Don't do this, Carly. I can be just as stubborn as you can, you know. I have the red hair to prove it!"

Reason had long since flown. She wanted only to lash out at him, to punish him for the despair that consumed her insides.

"If you show up, I'll have you arrested. I should probably do that anyway. The article says the SEC is investigating. Well, I, for one, will see they investigate you!"

"For the last time, will you hold your phone calls for five minutes to let me explain?" Desperation seemed to edge his tone.

"No!"

He bolted from the office, leaving Carly with fire burning in her throat. She would have her revenge at least. She dialed the number of the Securities and Exchange Commission. "I'm calling about the First Imperial case and a Mr. Richard Davis."

"One moment, please."

A masculine voice came on the line. "Mr. Davis is not handling that investigation any longer. Can I help you?"

ख

The rest of the day seemed endless. It ought to have gone quickly, because her phone never stopped ringing, and she handled three times as many transactions as normal, to say nothing of having to explain to those of her customers who still owned First Imperial what suspension in trading might mean to their accounts.

Finally, every buy and sell order, every pink telephone message, had been dealt with, and she realized the office had become very quiet. She rose and arched her back, feeling the tense muscles across her shoulders. She retrieved her purse, then walked silently through the large outer office and out glass doors onto Montgomery Street. The air was warmer than usual, and no fog hung over the tops of the skyscrapers. She pulled off her suit jacket and carried it over her arm while she walked to the cable car that would take her back to her apartment.

Being on the top floor, it had trapped the uncommon heat of the day, and she felt too warm. She undressed and slipped into shorts and a T-shirt. To make matters worse, the ache that had begun the moment she learned that Richard had been employed by the SEC would not go away. Yet she tried to push her agony to the back of her mind. She had to face it. She'd been too hasty to judge—had said things that now made her cringe.

She padded barefoot into the kitchen and opened her refrigerator. Nothing she saw appealed to her. She thought of all the cooking she'd done over the weekend and of all the meals she had eaten with Richard. *No,* she told herself, *I won't think about him.* Fighting down anger and regret, she sloughed back to the living room and plopped down on the window seat, where she let herself give way to weeping. What a fool she was. She'd been given another chance for love and had thrown it away in her usual impetuous fashion. Richard had done his best to answer her questions, and she had insisted on doubting him. Worse, she had refused to even let him explain.

Silent tears gave way to racking sobs, and she slipped off the window seat and knelt in front of it, resting her forehead on the padded seat. She began to pray. She asked God to forgive her for her faults and to help her overcome them. She prayed to understand His will for her and to be obedient from now on.

Finally, her crying stopped, but she felt exhausted, not only from the heat but from the turmoil in her thoughts. She got up and went to the wing chair, then saw the small stuffed bear Richard had won for her at the carnival on the Fourth of July. She untied the silk scarf from around its neck and put it on her own. Richard had joked that if he were a knight in a joust, the scarf would show that she was his lady fair. But she had spoiled her chance, and it was too late now to admit she would give anything to be Richard's lady.

seventeen

Carly wakened at her usual early hour the next day, although she'd fallen asleep lying across her bed, still wearing her shorts and the scarf Richard had given her. She dressed in her pink linen suit and again tied the silk scarf at her neck. The mix of pastel colors complemented the pink tones of her suit.

Her first call upon arriving at her office was from Mary Kemper, asking her to come to the Greenhouse Restaurant for lunch. Carly accepted. She wanted to ask the ladies a dozen questions. But after she asked the hostess for the Kemper sisters' table, she was taken to an empty booth. Richard's two aunts had not yet arrived. It wasn't like them to be late, but she only shrugged, sat down, and picked up the menu.

A tall figure approached and sat beside her.

Richard. His eyes were bloodshot, his jaw firm and hard. His gaze fell on the scarf at her throat, and his voice softened. "Don't get up. My aunts aren't coming. I'm sorry about the deception, but I had to see you, and I asked them to arrange it this way."

She had no intention of leaving. The sight of him seemed an answer to her prayers. She wanted to apologize but didn't know how to start.

"Carly, we can't have misunderstandings between us like this. When I left you yesterday, I called New York and got permission to tell you what's been going on."

"I called New York too. I know now that you work for the Securities and Exchange Commission. Oh, Richard, I'm so

162

ashamed for everything I said and did yesterday."

His eyes widened and then he slid closer to her in the booth and took both of her hands in his.

"Don't be. I should have told you all about it long ago."

"You tried to. I wouldn't let you. I was so angry."

He leaned closer and kissed her quickly, tenderly. "Carly, I've been in agony since yesterday. I've been trying to reassure myself that I haven't actually lied to you, but the fact is, I certainly never told you the whole truth."

The whole truth? Was there more? Carly felt as if the bottom might drop out of her world. She didn't want to hear anything that might threaten their love again. "You don't—"

"And not just today. So many times in these past weeks I've felt guilty about keeping you in the dark."

"Sometimes," she said, "you'd look at me with such sadness."

"But it's behind us now." He took a deep breath. "Here's the story. I've worked for the SEC for about five years. A few months ago, wanting to make a change, I looked around for something else. That's when Len Vickers called me."

"Then there is a link between Vickers and First Imperial?"

"Yes, and I'll get to it in a minute. This is a long story, but I'll try to keep it uncomplicated. First, a couple of months ago, Len called me from California and said he thought some unethical practices were going on in his company. Knowing I worked for the SEC, he asked some questions about unfriendly takeovers, and I told him what I knew. He didn't want us to investigate, but apparently I gave him enough information that he at least knew what to look for. He ousted one of the officers of his company, someone who stood to make a lot of money at Len's—and the company's—expense."

"Harold Yates? The man who resigned?"

"Yes, but that's not all."

"Go on."

A waitress came by to take their order, but Richard waved her away. "When he called to tell me he finally had it under control, he mentioned the name of a man who had been working with his unscrupulous officer—the name was Joel Unger."

"Your Joel Unger?" Carly said.

"The same. Except I hadn't begun to work with him at that time. I did discover, since I'd been thinking of changing jobs, that he needed another writer for his newsletter."

"But why did you go to work for him if you knew he'd been involved in the problem at Vickers Technology?"

"To investigate any further illegal activities. I wanted to put him out of business for good."

"For the SEC?"

"Yes—and no. I was in the midst of resigning by then. I took the job with Unger and immediately learned that he had an associate here on the West Coast who made a lot of contacts for him. I suspected he was the middleman between Unger and Vickers Technology. If I could find proof of the leak, I could keep it from happening again. That was the person I had to find. And I did. His next target was First Imperial. He would buy insider information and pass it through Unger."

"Printing it in his newsletter?"

"No, selling it to certain wealthy subscribers as a special service. Probably they didn't suspect he obtained it illegally, but the SEC will determine that. Lots of money can be made by anticipating dips and rises in the price of stocks."

Carly didn't interrupt but kept holding his hand.

"So I pretended ignorance and told Unger I wanted to open an office out here. Then I came out to find the man who was buying the insider information. I played the part of an investor looking for a hot tip and persuaded him to tell me how the scam worked. Last Friday, I mailed a list of names and a tape recording of my conversation with him, along with the tape of a later telephone call to Unger, to the SEC."

Things were making sense at last. "So that explains why you had a tape recorder in your bag at the Fourth of July festival."

"How did you know about that?"

"I saw it there when you went to get our dinner."

"We made an appointment to meet that day, and he contacted me while you were changing clothes."

"I saw you together when I came out, and you had your hand inside the bag. It looked odd. The man seemed so strange, I wondered what you were doing."

"You must have been very puzzled."

"Yes. Later I thought you were taping me. You even admitted it yesterday."

"I never taped any of our conversations, and I investigated you very briefly. Thanks to my years as a detective, I learned that your husband, Brett, had been the broker for Yates. I had to find out if he, or you, were profiting from insider information too."

"That explains all those questions about my attitude toward money." She looked into his eyes for confirmation.

"I exonerated you long before that. I learned right away that everything was aboveboard there. No, my sweet, I began investigating you for my own purposes." He paused and looked as if he wanted to kiss her again but, instead, rushed on, finishing his explanations. "I express-mailed the tapes on Friday, and they received them the next day."

"And the SEC suspended trading in the stock," she finished. "Will that straighten it all out and put the guilty people in jail?"

He shrugged. "Something like that. I'm sorry I couldn't

tell you all about it before, but it had to be done in secret."

"Just as I was sworn to secrecy by your aunts."

"Yes. I still don't know how they happened to sell the stock short. Must have been coincidence. I sometimes think they get their tips from a special guardian angel."

"Well, they didn't do anything illegal, did they?"

"No. I checked that out yesterday, after you told me about their short-selling. Their names were never mentioned. I intend to follow up and see to it that they're in no trouble. Besides, they don't know any of the officers or insiders of the company. As I said, it can only have been a coincidence, just as any investor might have bought or sold stock in the company. You had several other customers for the stock, didn't you?"

"Not many were left. Although I certainly never suggested that anyone sell short."

"It's not a bad technique, especially if you know in advance what's going to happen, like Joel Unger did."

"And he told you."

"Yes, but I didn't take advantage of it."

"You could have made a lot of money."

"SEC employees are under very strict rules about investing. That's one of the reasons I decided to resign."

"But you had resigned."

"That's true." A smile pulled at his lips.

"And you won't have a job with Unger anymore."

"No, I seem to be currently unemployed." However, his eyes twinkled with merriment. "Is that all right with you?"

"Anything you do is all right with me as long as you don't go away. You don't have to go back to New York, do you?"

"No, I'd never do that, unless you came with me. I'll find something out here."

"I'll support both of us, if necessary." The words seemed to leap out as if of their own accord, and Carly let go of his hand

and took a sip of water to cover her sudden nervousness.

"That is, if you still love me."

"You know I do."

"I'll never forgive myself for the way I behaved yesterday morning. But I hurt so much. I guess until then I hadn't let myself admit I could care this much for anyone."

"Are you used to the idea now?"

"Yes." She leaned against him, and he put one hand around her back. "Richard—"

"Yes, Love."

"I don't have to go back to the office until tomorrow morning. Can we spend the whole afternoon together?"

"And the evening," he added, pressing her closer. "From the first moment I saw you, I thought you were the most beautiful woman I'd seen in San Francisco, but I think it's the world."

"Stop! You'll make me blush."

"Will you marry me, Carly? I know I don't have a regular job, but I supported myself for years with investments."

For a long moment, she couldn't answer. Her moment of truth had come. Yet, no ambivalence clouded her judgment. She knew she was ready for this step. She had been for several days. She would always cherish the beautiful memory of Brett, but Richard was the future—an exciting, worthwhile future. "Yes," she said, her voice a whisper. "Oh, yes," she said, louder.

"Hooray!" The two feminine voices that had made the exclamation came from behind Carly.

She whirled around and saw two identical grins on the faces of Richard's two aunts, who were seated behind an enormous palm tree. Again, Carly was speechless.

"Congratulations," Mary Kemper said to her nephew, and the ladies pulled their chairs away from the protective cover of the shrubbery. "We knew you could do it!"

"And you must get married right away," Martha Kemper, added, "because we're not getting any younger, you know, and we want to see lots of red-headed great-nieces and nephews."

"Miss Kemper—" Carly began.

"Aunt Mary," Mary Kemper corrected. "We're going to be related now."

"Aunt Mary, you and Martha have been spying on us, haven't you?" Richard asked, pretending to be annoyed.

"No, of course not," Martha answered through smiling lips.

"We lunch here often," Mary added. "But I will admit," she giggled behind one hand, "when we arranged for you to be here—"

"—we asked for a table nearby," Martha finished.

"And now that you've found out," Richard continued, "I want to remind you of something else you've done recently—"

"Do you mean our selling short in First Imperial stock?"

"—and getting out before they stopped trading?" Martha added, then turned to her sister. "My, we had perfect timing, didn't we, Mary? Even we didn't think we'd be that good!"

"Just where did you get that stock tip to short-sell First Imperial?" Richard asked.

"Why, we got it from our book, of course. You remember, my dear," Mary turned to Carly for confirmation, "we told you we had read the most remarkable book about stock market timing."

"I remember." She had to turn her head from side to side again, as the ladies alternated speaking.

"Well," Martha continued, "that book told us about cycles, and we could see that First Imperial was ready for a down cycle, so we were supposed to sell short."

"We've never done that before," Mary added, "but it was a lot of fun."

"And very dangerous," Richard reminded them. "You could have lost a lot of money."

"I don't think so," Martha commented confidently. "If you follow the rules—"

"But you didn't know someone deliberately manipulated the stock. If you had delayed from Friday to Monday, you'd be in a much different position today."

"That was lucky," Mary admitted, "still, the rules said—"

"I can't contradict that." Richard shrugged and shook his head. "It's very hard to argue with success. But do be more careful in the future. Let Carly suggest stocks to you."

"Oh, we admit Carly's very good—" Mary began.

"But the fact is," Carly said, "you never asked me for a single stock suggestion. You've done very well without me. Perhaps I should take advice from you."

They all laughed, and Carly turned to Martha Kemper again. "There is one thing I want to know. Why did you wait so long to contact me? When my husband died, you didn't move your account or do any trading until Richard came to San Francisco."

"Well, Dear, we have a very good friend in our church who suggested we not rush into anything. We knew about your husband's tragic accident, and our friend told us to pray about it, to wait until we felt confident that the right time had come. Then Richard called us and said he had met you, and somehow we just knew that you were the person we were waiting for." She smiled a very smug, self-satisfied smile, then looked puzzled and apologetic, and turning to her sister, said, "Oh dear, I seem to have made a speech!"

Laughing with them, Carly said, "That's the first time I've

ever been the answer to anyone's prayers!"

Richard took his aunts' hands in his for a moment, then released them and touched Carly's cheeks in a tender gesture that told her how much he loved her. "You were only partly right. Carly is the person *I* was praying for!"

A Letter To Our Readers

Dear Reader:

In order that we might better contribute to your reading enjoyment, we would appreciate your taking a few minutes to respond to the following questions. We welcome your comments and read each form and letter we receive. When completed, please return to the following:

Rebecca Germany, Fiction Editor
Heartsong Presents
PO Box 719
Uhrichsville, Ohio 44683

1. Did you enjoy reading *Charade* by Phyllis Humphrey?
   ☐ Very much! I would like to see more books
   by this author!
   ☐ Moderately. I would have enjoyed it more if
   _____
   _____
   _____

2. Are you a member of **Heartsong Presents**? Yes ☐ No ☐
   If no, where did you purchase this book?_____
   _____

3. How would you rate, on a scale from 1 (poor) to 5 (superior), the cover design?_____

4. On a scale from 1 (poor) to 10 (superior), please rate the following elements.

   _____ Heroine   _____ Plot

   _____ Hero   _____ Inspirational theme

   _____ Setting   _____ Secondary characters

5. These characters were special because_____

_____

_____

6. How has this book inspired your life?_____

_____

_____

7. What settings would you like to see covered in future
   Heartsong Presents books?_____

_____

_____

8. What are some inspirational themes you would like to see
   treated in future books?_____

_____

_____

9. Would you be interested in reading other **Heartsong
   Presents** titles?   Yes ❏   No ❏

10. Please check your age range:
    ❏ Under 18   ❏ 18-24   ❏ 25-34
    ❏ 35-45   ❏ 46-55   ❏ Over 55

Name _____

Occupation _____

Address _____

City _____ State _____ Zip _____

Email _____

Seattle

Shepherd of Love Hospital stands as a beacon of hope in Seattle, Washington. Its Christian staff members work with each other—and with God—to care for the sick and injured. But sometimes they find their own lives in need of a healing touch.

Can those who heal find healing for their own souls? How will the Shepherd for whom their hospital is named reveal the love each longs for?

Titles by Colleen L. Reece

Lamp in Darkness
Flickering Flames
Kindled Spark
Hearth of Fire

paperback, 352 pages, 5 ³⁄₁₆" x 8"

♥ ♥ ♥ ♥ ♥ ♥ ♥ ♥ ♥ ♥ ♥ ♥ ♥ ♥

♥ ♥ ♥ ♥ ♥ ♥ ♥ ♥ ♥ ♥ ♥ ♥ ♥ ♥

····Hearts♥ng····

HEARTSONG PRESENTS *TITLES AVAILABLE NOW:*

·······Presents·······